THE WAITE FAMILY
BOOK 3

KATHI S. BARTON

World Castle Publishing, LLC
Pensacola, Florida
Copyright © Kathi S. Barton 2012
Print ISBN: 9781938243912
eBook ISBN: 9781938243929
First Edition World Castle Publishing LLC July 15, 2012
http://www.worldcastlepublishing.com
Licensing Notes
Cover: Karen Fuller
Photos: Shutterstock
Editor: Brieanna Robertson

~Chapter 1~

Lieutenant Colonel David Patterson hopped from the chopper while it was still a good three feet from landing. Bending his considerable frame over to avoid losing his head, David made his way to the group of men who appeared to be sitting around a large table. Saluting to men he passed as if his hand were a rapier slicing through the air, David stopped in front of them. He could hear his bodyguards scrambling up the hill after him.

"You hear anything yet?" No one moved. No one at the table even acknowledged his presence. "Have you found my man yet?" he asked again. Still not a word. Then one of the men raised his hand up off the table slightly and pointed to just behind David.

The soldier standing there was huge. Probably six-foot-six, he looked as if he lifted trees the size of the one he was leaning against for weight training. The M-16 across his massive chest looked smaller than David knew the rifle to actually be. His shirt was open and his pants, Army issued fatigues, looked dirty and stained. David turned to him and took one step.

David never heard the person move, not a whisper of sound or a slight shift in the air surrounding them. But he could feel him. His hand around David's chest was hot even through his shirt. But it was the sharp bite of the blade at David's throat that had him hold all movement. When he swallowed the blade bit into his skin and soon he felt a small trickle of what he assumed was his blood make its way down his throat. He slowly raised his hands, palms up and out.

The whispered "don't" from the man in front of him had David stop. He wasn't sure if he had been talking to David or the man behind him. A slight scuffle behind him made him wish he had waited for his escort.

"I'm Lieutenant Colonel Pat—"

"I know who you are. Are you with those idiots or on your own?" The blade at his throat relaxed just a bit when the man with the rifle nodded. David didn't relax, but he did breathe just a little deeper. "Captain Waite called me yesterday. She said her men…Shipley?" At the man's nod, David continued. "She said her men were in trouble. That something was…not right." The man snorted.

If he knew his captain then he probably realized she said a great deal more than things not being right. She'd actually told him that things were "fucked up" and that she was going to have to "kill a few cock-suckers" before this was over. Captain Waite had a way with words.

The blade disappeared suddenly and David found himself being shoved toward a hut. The man with the rifle, Sergeant Roger Shipley, just ahead of him, was leading the way.

In the hut were seven men, a map laid out in front of them, and several weapons lying about the floor and chairs. David would bet these were the weapons the men at the table outside the hut had been armed with. He said nothing as the other men stood and saluted and then went back to the map.

"Captain Waite was supposed to check in every five— standard for this type of operation. She sometimes misses one, call of nature, but when she missed two we went on alert," one of the men said to the room in general.

David moved two Glocks to the floor and sat down close to the table. Shipley did the same. David looked over the map table and frowned.

"I talked to her at zero-six hundred yesterday. How long has she been out of contact?"

"Six hours, thirty-two minutes," Shipley said after consulting his watch. "Those yahoos out there showed up an hour ago. Said they were here to debrief and replace. Said Capt was dead and we were to…Barnhart? What they tell you?"

A man nearly as large as Shipley stood up and grinned. "Said Capt was dead and we were to 'cease and desist.' We ceased their mother fucking asses and had no more need for their desistance."

David smiled. He was sure that went over well. "Did they tell you why or who sent them?"

"You did," Shipley said as he looked at the man who just rushed in the door. Every man in the room drew their weapon too. David was shoved to the floor.

"Found her. She's…it's bad, sarge. Real bad."

David followed the men. He had thought about asking for them to bring a medic along, but he could see that Shipley was ahead of him on that score too. They were all running at full march across a forest and not making a sound. When they came upon a soldier on his knees in the dirt they slowed. Shipley and the medic stepped forward. When David started to follow he was stopped by a gun to his chest. He looked around. Bodies, not just the one they were going to, but others, several others. At least four, maybe five

David wasn't a stupid man. And he wasn't a stupid leader. He could see that something had these men on full alert even if one didn't take into consideration the phone call he'd gotten yesterday morning from Sin…

"David, my team is being deployed again. What the fuck is the matter with you people? I told you cock suckers no more without R&R. Are you stupid down there in Washington?"

Sydney was nothing if not direct. David sat in his kitchen booth in his home and tried to understand why she was calling him and not her commanding officer. She continued before he could ask.

"'Cause I gotta tell you, if I don't have some down time soon somebody's dick is coming off right up to his nuts and then some."

He cringed at the image. "Where are you being deployed to? Last I heard you were in Spain on your three week furlough. Who gave the orders this time?"

There was a great deal of static then he heard other voices. When she came through again David was glad he was sitting down.

"You did." David dropped his mug of coffee. *"Orders say we are to go to Morocco and await further orders. Damn it, David, we just go back from a seven mouth turn. My men are beat to hell and back. We needed this."*

"I didn't send you." He had to think. Morocco. What the hell was in Morocco? Nothing that he could think of that would send his best re-con team there. *"When do you leave? And from where?"*

"We're boarding as we speak. Took our cells and personals." The static was harsher this time, louder. *"Not liking this, David. Some bullshit is going down and my men are fubared if this plays out like I'm thinking it will."*

FUBAR—Fucked Up Beyond All Recognition. Taking their personals meant they'd have nothing—no clothes, medical packs or anything. They were being dropped. Then he realized she was speaking to someone else.

"...take a piss? What the fuck, you expect me to hang it out the chopper bay and hope it lands on an unfriendly? Fuck off, buddy. I don't have the equipment to even make that remotely possible. I could try by pissing on your head." A short, sharp reply, then, *"Yeah, I thought so too."*

Sydney was very ladylike too, David thought.

Her voice was low and urgent. *"We're in Madrid. The chopper leaves in ten, unless I need a shit too. Then we rendezvous with a ship out at sea. You tell me you had nothing to do with this and I'll expect you to save my men."*

"I didn't, I swear it. I'm coming. I'll meet you in Morocco tomorrow night. Keep me informed." He was

rushing to his bedroom as he spoke. He didn't have a lot of time.

"And just how the fuck do you expect me to do that? Carrier pigeon? I'll try and send out some smoke signals. Dumb fuck." He heard her take a deep breath and that, more than anything, scared him. *"Just make sure you keep your promise. If you don't, then I'm fucking coming back to castrate your fucking ass."* The line went dead.

And Sydney had a way with words that made one weep.

David had left immediately for the airport. For whatever reason, he didn't want to think about flying service. He felt in his gut it wasn't smart. He got the next flight to Africa then rented a chopper to the nearest military base. That was how he had ended up here in the middle of nowhere with a missing man.

Halfway there he'd heard someone over the radio saying that Captain Waite was missing and then presumed dead. He didn't believe the latter of the two messages. He knew that she was alive. It was all David could do not to jump in the pilot's seat and fly himself. Now she was found and in bad shape.

"Colonel? She…she wants to speak to you." The man holding him back stepped away and David moved forward. He could smell the blood about four or so feet from her. It wasn't until Shipley moved for him that David saw her.

"Christ," he hissed.

Her short hair was red, bloodied red. David could see a trickle of blood coming from her left ear. Her left eye was swollen completely shut and a large cut ran the length of her brow. It looked to be to the skull. Her nose was bent at an angle and her cheek was opened wide. Her right eye was open, but he doubted she could see much from it. It was filled with blood and it seeped from the corner. Her mouth was moving, but David couldn't understand her yet. He knelt down to her. There was a medic working on her chest.

The blood was pooling too fast for him to be sure, but it looked like five bullet holes along her right side and one more in her belly. The medic was working frantically to stop the bleeding. Her left arm was broken; David could see her bone sticking through her forearm. Looking down her body he could see the destruction went to her legs, as both were broken it appeared. He leaned closer still when she continued to whisper.

"Promised," she said. "Keep promise."

David felt tears burn his eyes. "You aren't going to die, damn it. I won't have it. Buck up, captain, or I'll have your bars." David could feel the tears fall. There was no way she was going to live through this and they all knew it.

"Promise."

Sydney coughed then and blood poured from her mouth. David was suddenly shoved out of the way as the medic that had come with them worked to save her.

David leaned back on his heels and did something he'd not done since his wife passed away three years before. He prayed. Prayed to God that Sydney Waite made it.

~~~

Cain was sitting in his office looking at the file of his newest patient. All seven pounds, three ounces of her. Mary Margaret Turner had been born at two-fifteen this morning and everyone was doing fine. Cain couldn't help but feel pride in what he'd been able to do. Had he not been at the hospital when he had both mother and daughter wouldn't have made it. The car accident they'd been in would have cut both their lives short. Cain leaned back in his chair and closed his eyes.

When his phone rang on his desk he let it go. He wasn't officially here. He didn't need to be at the office for another hour and he was taking a short nap to keep him from falling asleep while he did rounds. Besides, if his family needed him they had his—

The cell in his pocket vibrated. He smiled. Only his wife or his sisters were the only ones with this number. He hoped it was Alyssa, his wife. He reached into his pocket and answered without looking at the caller ID.

"Hello, sweetheart."

The silence at the other end startled him. Then he thought it was indeed one of his sisters or maybe his brother-in-law. He grinned when he thought of Drew being called "sweetheart."

"Doctor Waite, Cain Waite?"

Cain sat up in his chair. Terror had his heart pounding. No matter who was at the other end, this could not be good news.

"Yes. Yes, this is Cain Waite. What's happened?" Silence again.

"My name is Patterson, Lieutenant Colonel David Patterson. I'm...I know your sister, Captain Sy...Christ."

Cain closed his eyes when he heard the man sob.

Sydney was dead. He knew it as surely as Patterson had already told him. He reached for his desk phone to dial his wife. He didn't know how he'd manage it with two phones when someone knocked on his door. Standing, he opened it as the man on the phone began speaking again.

"There's been a...I'm not even sure what happened. She's hurt, your sister. She's been beaten and shot and they're taking her to the closest M.A.S.H. unit now. Then from there...fuck, I don't know."

Cain leaned against the door jamb and felt his knees tremble. *Not dead, not dead,* kept running through his head. He looked up at the nurse standing there and drew a complete blank on her name.

"Call my wife. I need her. Tell her...tell her to come here now. Tell her Sin's been hurt." Then Cain turned to the phone. "Patterson...her boss, or whatever. She talked about you. Said...she said that you...where is my sister?"

"They are taking her by my chopper out now. We should land in...hang on." Cain heard him speaking to someone else. It was then that Cain could hear the *whoop-whoop* of chopper blades. "She is going to be taken to Guelmim Military Air Base in Southern Morocco. From there...I don't give a good fuck what you think I can or can't give him. See these bars?" Raised voices then Patterson was back. "Sorry. From the base we're e-vac'ing her out ASAP to a hospital ship in the Atlantic. I'm pulling in all the favors I can to get you to her, but I can't get you on the ship. Closest I can get you is...I'm sorry, Waite, the closest I can get you is New York."

There was quiet now. Almost eerie quiet and Cain thought he'd lost the call. Then he head a toilet flush then a door shut. He strained to hear something, anything when Patterson came back, his voice full of emotion and low now.

"Waite and I had a deal. She gets hurt enough where…where she might die and I was to call you. She wanted you to know. 'No sugar coat,' she said, 'you tell Cain like its gospel.'" Another sob, then, "It's bad, Waite, I'm not going to lie to you. It's real bad. They don't…she might not make it to the M.A.S.H. much less to the ship. I'm doing…she'd been shot. She…Christ, what they did to her."

Cain dropped to the floor. He simply couldn't stand any longer. His desk phone was ringing and he could only stare at it. Nothing was getting through. He knew that Patterson was speaking still, but he couldn't focus, couldn't seem to grasp what he was saying. When a nurse came to him she was speaking, but he simply stared at her. Then he felt the room tilt and he was out.

~Chapter 2~

Cain and Alyssa moved among the officers and servicemen who were onboard the ship—hospital ship, actually. Alyssa was looking for the person in charge and for Patterson. She didn't know whether to shoot him or hug him when she found him.

When she'd gotten to Cain's office he'd been cussing a blue streak. Some of the words he'd strung together still made her smile. He could be quite inventive when the mood struck him, she realized. But as soon as he'd seen her he'd pulled her into his arms and held her to him. She started to tell him to let her breathe, but the look on Marsha's face had her stop. Something had happened.

"They won't...Sin's been shot and beat up. I was talking to her boss...some lieutenant or something—Patterson. That was it. He said...we can only go to New York then I don't know...I need to..." Cain held her as he cried.

Forty minutes later she was on the phone to someone that could help. Her father had made great contacts when he'd been alive and she had been working on reestablishing them since she'd been running Howard Corporation. When she'd told the President what she needed the Waite family was on board a jet bound for Washington. Then a short helicopter ride out to sea to the ship that Sydney was being treated on. They had arrived an hour ago.

"Mrs. Howard? My name is Ensign Charles. I'm to take you to the receiving room. The colonel is there along with the commander of this vessel. They will meet you there."

"Thank you, ensign. And it's Waite, not Howard. I'm married." Cain took her hand as they followed the young man down the long hallway.

The room they were shown to was lovely. Alyssa didn't think one would be able to tell it was a room on a huge ship. There were several sitting areas and a long couch. There was even a fireplace. After they were left alone Quinn and Drew took one area and Cain paced. He'd been doing that a great deal over the past several hours.

"What the hell is taking so long? I want to see Sin, not sit around waiting for someone to get around to us." That was another thing he'd been doing, snapping at people.

"Cain, why don't you just have—"

"I don't want to sit down. I want to see Sin. Now."

Okay, she'd had enough. "You either sit your ass down on that couch right now, buster, or I'll put you there. And the next time you use that tone with me I'll snap your dick off so quick you won't know what happened." Alyssa pointed to the couch. "Sit!"

He sat, but he didn't do it without some grumbling. She didn't care so long as he sat down. She needed to take a breath too. When the door opened and three men walked in Cain started to rise, but sat back down. She went to him and held his hand.

"Doctor and Mrs. Waite? I'm Lieutenant Colonel Patterson. This is the commander of this ship, Commander Welsh, and Doctor Keller. Please have a seat."

Cain stood up and watched Quinn walk to them. She was seven months pregnant with triplets and Cain hadn't wanted her to come. Alyssa smiled when she thought of the temper Quinn had and hoped she'd see it more. She and Quinn had gone through their pregnancy together until Alyssa had given birth to hers and Cain's little boy, Connor, a few weeks ago. She looked over to where he was sleeping in the carrier Cain had sat on the end of the couch.

"This is another sister, Quinn Miller, and her husband Andrew Miller. My sisters Grace Ann and Lilliane are enroute and Jasmine is coming with them later." Cain flushed. "I'm sorry. I'm babbling. Please, tell us how Sin is."

Doctor Keller cleared his throat. "She's alive, though I don't have a clue why. By all rights…I'm sorry. I tend to speak my mind. But that girl should have died in that fucking jungle. Beg pardon, ladies."

Alyssa smiled. "Don't worry. Just speak your mind. My husband is a doctor too. I think we'd all like to hear what you have to say." They all nodded. "Please, go on."

"Captain Waite was shot seven times—five to the chest, one lower abdomen, one to the right shoulder. The ones to her chest missed her heart by a hair's breadth, and I do mean it was close. One centimeter to the right and she'd be dead. Probably only thing that saved her were the field medics. Patterson here said they were all over her when they found her. Those boys…they don't get enough credit for what they do over there."

Alyssa held Cain's hand tighter as the doctor continued. "Like I said, she'd lost a good deal of her blood. Took seven units to top off her tank, then we had some standing by just in case. She won't like it, but there you have it. Heard tell she had one of them cards in her file that said nothing heroic." He laughed. "Guess if her men knew about it, they plum forgot about it."

Alyssa was sure that they hadn't. She looked over at Patterson and she knew he was aware of it too. Neither Cain nor Quinn knew, though, she could tell. Both wore identical expressions of disbelief.

"When can we see her?" Cain was squeezing her hand tightly now and she was going to lose fingers if he didn't let go. "I think my husband and the rest of us need to be sure."

Cain stood up and kissed her hand that he'd been abusing. "I'd also like to see her medical chart and confer with the surgeon. Is there a place my sister can rest? She shouldn't—"

A growl behind him stopped him and Alyssa laughed. Oh yeah, this Quinn was going to be much more fun than the pre-pregnant one.

~~~

Cain watched her breathing. In and out, in and out. He knew that she really had no choice in the matter being hooked up to a ventilator, but it still gave him comfort to see her chest rise and fall like it did. He'd been watching her for over an hour now and he still couldn't bring himself to look beyond her breathing. But he did glance down at the chart in his hands.

He couldn't seem to make himself open it either. It would solve a lot of his questions, but Sin was his baby sister, the baby to them all, and to have her looking like this, pale and wrapped up the way she was, it was nearly too much for him. When the door to her room opened then closed, he didn't even turn to see who it was.

"I feel as if I know you." David sat in one of the chairs; the sound of the air going out of the cushion was loud in the room. "She talked about her family all the time."

"She told us that you were her friend and that she wouldn't have gotten this far without you saving her bottom a few times." Cain looked at his sister's face. "I don't feel much like thanking you for that right now."

He heard the man snort. "I don't like me much for it right now either. She's a hell of a girl, but she has a small problem with…let's just say that I've noticed it seems to be a trait in your family to speak your minds."

Cain smiled, remembering his wife having a word with Commander Welsh just about an hour ago. She'd torn a strip of hide off the man Cain was sure he'd feel every time he sat down. He loved Alyssa more every day.

"What do you mean you can't do much more for her? You will do everything in your power to make sure she lives or I will find someone who will. I'm not going to have to go above your head, am I?" Alyssa had been

nursing Connor and looked very Madonnalike sitting there.

"Yes, ma'am. No, ma'am. That is to say...Captain Waite has a DNR. We can't go beyond that for her. You understand." Welsh wiped the sweat from his brow and looked over at Cain. He just shrugged. He would let her handle this. She was better at it anyway.

"And that means what to me?" She lifted the blanket and adjusted herself. Cain started to tell her what it meant, but was cut off by Welsh.

"It means Do Not Resuscitate. We can't do anything heroic to—"

"I'm well aware of what DNR means, you dolt. My husband is a top notch physician." She stood now and so did Welsh. "You will do everything in your power to save my sister or, so help me, I will have you busted back down to a buck private in three minutes. Do I make myself clear?"

"We don't have buck pri... Yes, ma'am, I will remove that from her file as soon as I get back to her room. And I will make sure that she has the utmost best care that I can...the Navy can give her."

Commander Welsh looked as though he was going to say something else, but left in a big hurry. Cain had no doubt he had not only removed the offending sheet from her file, but had made sure that every man and woman on that ship knew that Sydney Waite was cared for as if she were the President.

"He crumbled very quickly, didn't he? Do you think it wise to have a man who would give up so easily in charge *of our fighting men and woman?" she asked as the door closed behind the commander.*

Cain pulled her into his arms, baby and all. "I think he thought you were scarier than even the worst enemy. You should think about advising the President on how to run his army. Might be fun to watch."

That had been two days ago. Now Cain was sitting in the room with his sister who was hooked up to every known piece of medical equipment known to man and then some.

"Cain, what if…she's not going to be able to come back to the service you know. There was too much…the damage was too much. They won't let her come back."

Cain had figured that. He'd heard a few of the others talking about her retirement. Cain wasn't sure how Sin would take it, but he knew it wouldn't be pretty. He wasn't going to tell her either. That wasn't his job. He glanced over at David.

"Do you know what happened yet?"

David didn't say anything for a few minutes. "No, not really. We are looking into it with the utmost care. Whatever the fuck that means. I have my own team of people looking into it. Some of her own men, too, are helping me out."

Neither man said anything for awhile longer then David said he needed to find the commander. David said he was expecting someone soon. Cain nodded.

It was time, he knew it. He opened the file and immediately shut it again. It took him several more minutes to reopen it and actually begin to read. After two hours he knew that he would have nightmares about the file's contents for the rest of his life if not beyond. He sat back in his chair and cried. Then found his wife and cried some more.

~Chapter 3~

Sin watched the men in front of her. Not one of them had said a word since she'd told them what the doctor had told her. Well...most of what the doctor had told her. The rest, it was personal.

"But you'll be back, right?" Harley Johnson was a good man and she loved having him on her team, but there were times, like now, that she wondered how he knew to breathe in and out all the time.

"Do you have any brain cells at all in that noggin of yours? She just said she was mustering out." They knocked him around good naturedly before Shipley whistled. Silence reigned.

"No, Johnson, I'm...I'm finished. I've been too long in the field anyway and they want someone younger to take over." Sin glanced at Shipley. Her sergeant was the only one who knew the real truth.

Sydney Waite was being Honorably Discharged with full pay and benefits. Hell, even the President had been by to give her a Purple Heart and her Gold Star. She was also up for the Congressional Medal of Honor. All thanks to the men before her. Each and every one of them had put in a request to honor her. Even David Patterson had sent in a less than cordial request.

She smiled when she thought about him telling her. "It's the least they can flipping do. Damned bureaucrats sitting up there in that flipping office sending you to who knows where to be shot up and then beat to heck and back. Why, if I had an ounce of sense, I'd retire right this blessed moment." David had been worked up, but not enough to let go with some real cussing. His late wife had asked him not to speak like he lived in a gutter and Sin had only heard him let go of that tight hold once in all the time she'd known him.

"Hopefully she'll be prettier. Gotta tell ya, Capt, you look like shit. I mean, for all that's happened…well, you was passable. Now? Not so much. You might have to settle down with ugly old Barnes here now. I know he ain't much, but he might'n be all you can count on to take you. And we all know he ain't par-tick-u-lar." She laughed just as Morgan had wanted her to.

But only a few of them, Shipley being one, could see that it didn't reach her eyes. The truth was, she wished she'd died out there in that field all those months ago and only now was wondering why she hadn't.

Her men…well, the men bantered around for another twenty minutes or so until the nurses ran them off. They'd been getting progressively louder as they stood there. And while she was used to their language she was sure that others were not.

"You gonna be all right, Capt? I can still take you back to Ohio with me. Can't say there's anything keeping me here anymore." Shipley sat backwards on the only chair in the room and leaned against the back of it, his massive arms crossed.

He'd told her yesterday that he was out too. Roger Shipley said he couldn't go back. Not now. He wouldn't trust them anyways and he, too, had taken the retirement just like she had. The only difference was she was forced to and he wasn't.

"Nah, I'll be fine. I'm going to go and stay with my brother and his wife for a little while before I move on. He has this cabin thing he said I could stay in for as long as I want. He and his wife have a kid about nine months old now. Might not be too bad."

Shipley snorted. He knew she didn't know squat about rug rats. He'd told her once she went from infant to adult in a matter of hours. Said he'd never met anyone as young as her that was as mature. She had never been sure if he was having fun with her or not. She'd let it go without asking.

"They'll have you changing diapers in a heartbeat, Capt. I think I'd pay good money to see that, you with poop on your clothes and up-chuck on your face."

She smiled. Not going to happen. She knew that Shipley was going to go and visit his family in Canada. He had a kid or two up there. He'd been divorced for so long that he'd told her once he couldn't remember what they looked like. But he'd give it a go. Then he was going to go home to his place in the Bayou. He had a big house down there that he'd had built when he'd gotten his second bonus a few years ago.

After a few minutes more he left. He'd wanted something from her…she had no idea what, but she could tell. He'd never been a very talkative man; none of them had been really, especially when they were out in the field. But they'd been together for the better part of ten years, fifty if you counted service time the way it felt. But they had to move on from here. So with a hearty handshake, he left.

Sin had joined the Army just before her senior year in high school. She'd been sixteen when she'd signed up. She hadn't even had to forge her father's signature. He'd been more than willing to have her gone from the house sooner than necessary. She'd not been able to afford college and, unlike her brother Cain, her grades were never good enough for anything other than community college anyway. She knew she couldn't live at home anymore so she had Roscoe sign her paperwork and, the day she'd turned eighteen, she'd left on a bus to Texas without a backward glance.

She loved the rigid rules and the tight way things were done. It was organized with a defined set of regulations that she followed to the letter. Well, most of the time. She'd moved up the ranks quickly until she reached captain and since she'd loved that so much, she'd stayed there.

Sin could fire her weapon and just about anything else they'd put before her with superior skills. She'd been excellent as an officer and she knew that in the past few years she'd managed to not step on too many toes. She hoped.

Once out of boot camp she excelled in military training, beating every other team out on drills. That was where she'd met most of her team, during one of those first drills. They'd made her the leader and had followed her all the way, making them the most winning team in all the Army. She'd also met David Patterson.

He'd been married then. His wife, Charlotte Patterson, had been a quiet and reserved woman who would only need to frown a bit to have either of them scrambling to do whatever it took to make her smile. Sin had spent plenty of Friday nights at their house, eating dinner and arguing over something stupid. Mrs. Patterson had been more a mother to her than her own had ever been. She missed the woman a great deal.

"Well, kid." David had been her drill sergeant then. "Looks like I've been assigned to make a man outta you. What do you think about that?"

"I think my tits might get in the way, but hey, who knows?" She could still remember the shocked look on his face then the bright redness. She'd thought she'd gone too far, but he proved to be just as lippy as she was.

"Might," he said as he glanced down at her large boobs. "But maybe we can get 'em strapped down with some duct tape. If that don't fix it that just means we haven't used enough."

Sin simply stared at him. She'd never heard that expression before and wasn't sure if he had meant to actually do it. When he burst out laughing she joined him. That had earned her two hundred push-ups and a week on KP duty. It didn't curb her tongue, but it did make her respect him more. And they became good friends. And every time David got a promotion he took Sin right along with him, kicking and screaming all the way. Up until the last time.

When Charlotte was ill, Sin had just been promoted to captain. David had decided to retire. They offered him the position of lieutenant colonel and his wife told him to take it. Sin was sure that was the only thing that had kept him from going off the deep end and eating a bullet when she finally succumbed to cancer.

And now she was headed home and he had another year to go on his twenty-five years before he would retire with full honor. Sin thought she just might miss him most of all. She laid her head back on the pillow and closed her eyes.

In five days she would be home. She was going straight to her brother's house for a few days then to the house where she would live until she figured out what to do with herself. She was twenty-seven years old, single and, thanks to a bunch of metal holding her together, she could set off metal detectors all over the place. Opening her eyes, she decided that she couldn't feel sorry for herself here and moved to the edge of the bed.

Sin got up slowly, moved over to the chair that Shipley had been sitting in, and sat down gingerly. The wheel chair was there for her to use. But she had been determined to get around on her own without it since she'd ridden down the halls the first time five weeks ago. It made her feel ridiculous and stupid. The next day she was at the PT room three times. And more every day until she could walk on her own.

When the door opened behind her she didn't even bother turning around. She just knew it was one of the MP's again, asking her if she needed anything. She decided to cut him off before she murdered him.

"No. I do not need you to pick me up anything from the mess hall, nor do I require you to get me anything from the store. I'm perfectly fine just the way I am. If you do happen to run into a male stripper or two, now *that* I could use."

"I wouldn't bring you a stripper if I could, you're much too young. I know you're fine, you're too fucking stubborn to be otherwise and, well, I guess you don't want us to give you a lift home then, huh?"

She turned and looked at her brother and promptly burst into tears.

~Chapter 4~

Payton Cooperider knew he was going to die if he didn't get help soon. He never expected things to go so badly as quickly as they had today. He was on a filthy back alley in the worst part of town. He looked down at the blood pouring from the wound in his leg. He supposed that was nothing compared to the one in his gut.

Coop laid his head back and tried to remember what the hell he'd been thinking in becoming a cop then moving up the slippery ladder until he made detective. He'd never been one for rules and wondered how he'd taken a job where he'd had to enforce them. Dumbass, was all he could think. Coop coughed hard and blood splattered on his chest.

"Not good, Coop, not good at all." He didn't realize he'd spoken out loud until the rat across the way from him sat up and glared at him. "Fuck! My last confession is gonna be heard by a rat. Well…guess that's about like anyone else I know." The rat scurried off. "Traitor," Coop said softly as his radio squawked.

"Dead yet, Cooperider? You could certainly do us all a big favor if you just stop breathing."

Coop froze at the voice at the other end of his radio. "Captain?"

Laughter erupted from the ear piece. "Course if you die in the next twenty minutes then you'll still be on duty. Nice to die with full honors, even for a putz like you."

Coop had to be drifting in and out of consciousness and hadn't realized he wasn't getting the help he'd radioed for. He pulled out his own cell phone and realized he'd radioed for help, officer down nearly an hour ago. Fuck, he was a dead man. His captain, Carl Wickett, spoke again.

"Just knew you'd follow orders. Ain't nothing but consistent are you, Cooperider? Well, I had you leave that fancy cell of yours at home so in the event something…oh I don't know, like you getting gut shot happened, then you'd be too hurt to ask for help."

Coop wiped the blood off his hands onto his pants legs of his jeans as he opened his phone to text. There was only one person he knew he could trust right now and he hoped she wasn't somewhere that it would take her too long to get to her only boy.

"You there, Cooperider? Did you wonder why I gave you that fancy phone thing to wear?" He had, but didn't answer. "I got that from the powers that be. They said to make sure you had a nice policeman's funeral and I aim to please."

"Yeah, you always were great at ass kissing." Coop hit send and made his voice lower, weaker. "Powers that be,

huh? So the chief wants me dead, huh? Wonder when—"
A coughing fit cut him off.

"Oh that sounds really bad, Cooperider. You should
see a doctor before that kills you. Chief? Nah, not him. He
actually likes your goody-two-shoes ass. Nah, this goes
higher than that. Might find me sitting next to the mayor if
you weren't dying."

Coop's phone vibrated. "*Coming,*" it said. Then
seconds later, "*You die and I will personally kick your ass,
young man.*" Then another, "*I love you, son.*"

He closed his eyes. Mom was coming. And she would
kick his ass if he died, he thought with a grin. Coughing
again, he hoped he could hang on for her. He really would
hate to disappoint her. But for now he needed information.
He dialed a second number, this time a phone number and
not as a text.

When the voice at the other end answered Coop spoke
quickly. "Mayor Chaney? Wow, you must have sucked a
lot of dick to get that kind of job. So you think me and the
chief are expendable do you, Wickett?"

Another burst of laughter. "Expendable is a good
word. College didn't do you a damn bit of good, do you
think? You're still bleeding to death in a dirty alley with
only rats to keep you company."

It occurred to Coop that he might not have anyone on
the call and he'd been hung up on when he hadn't
answered right away. He tried to lift the phone and had
tried several times, but he was too weak and he'd lost too
much blood.

"I'll take my life over yours any day of the week,
Wickett." Coop saw a shadow moving toward him. It

blurred in and out before he could make it out. "Mom, is that you?"

"Damn, boy, seeing your mama before you bite the big one? You really are a putz. A rich, dead, fucking putz." The radio went off on a bite of laughter.

Coop smiled up at his mom. "I think the chief is on my phone if the rat didn't take it with him when he left."

"Oh, Payton, whatever have you gotten yourself into? I have the medical team on the way. Let me have that phone, son."

Coop couldn't seem to make his fingers loosen their grip. Then he saw two more people there and he sort of fuzzed out. Next thing he knew, he was in a moving vehicle.

"Detective Cooperider? You're going to be fine. We're life-flighting you to the doctors now. Can you tell me where you hurt the worst?"

His tongue felt thick and his mouth dry. He hurt everywhere, he wanted to scream at him, but couldn't manage it. Closing his eyes, he tried to concentrate on the exact location of each pain, but he must have fuzzed out again because he was in a more stationary bed and he was looking at a pretty girl.

"Mom?"

She grinned at him. "Hardly, detective. I'm Doctor Rosa. We're going to take you to surgery as soon as we land. You've lost a good deal of blood, but I want you to stay with us." She stepped out of his sight then came back. "Oh, your chief…huh, Cramer, Allen Cramer, said to tell you they got the bad guys."

Coop felt his body begin to float. He must have made some noise because he heard someone tell him it was an IV.

~~~

It was four weeks to the day and he was bored. Not just bored, but if Coop had one more person ask him if he was feeling all right he may beg someone to bring him his gun in and start shooting them. He knew he was lucky to be alive. Hell, everyone from the woman who came in and mopped up his floor to the doctors kept telling him how lucky he'd been. But he still couldn't get over the fact that someone had planned his death. Not just planned it, but had been there when they thought he'd been going to bite the big one.

His leg had taken the longest to heal. The bullet had gone straight through the large muscle in his calf and had done some major damage. He'd had to have physical therapy three times a week just to be able to bend his knee. And now he had to go and learn to walk on it again. Well, not learn he supposed, but how to walk on it so that he would strengthen the muscles without doing more harm than good. He'd come back to his room covered in sweat and wanted something for the pain the first two days. Less drugs, but no less sweat after that.

He looked at the television and finally just shut it off with a growl.

"Behave, young man. Don't make me have to bring in that nice nurse again and set you straight."

Coop started to glare at his mom, but she raised that brow of hers and he stopped. He respected his mom. Loved her with all of his heart. She'd done all right for them since his dad had died, but hell, she could scare him near to death when she wanted to.

"Shouldn't you be at some meeting or something? I bet you have a sh...crap load of other things to do besides hand sit with me. I wouldn't want to sit with me. I'm cranky." He was a hell of a lot more than cranky, but he wouldn't tell his mom that.

She stood up and poured him a cup of water. "Drink. And I have nothing to do at the moment." She fussed with the pillows under his leg, the one that the bullet had ripped through. He reached down and grabbed her hand.

"Mom? What is it?" Every time he woke up over the past two weeks she'd been right there by his bed. Sometimes his sister Shaller, but always her.

"You scared me, Payton. When I got that text from you...what if I had turned off my phone? What if I been further away and not made it? What if—"

"You can 'what if' things all day, but the simple truth is none of those things happened." He kissed her hand as he continued. "You didn't turn off your phone and you weren't too far away and you made it. That's all you need to remember."

With another pat to the pillow she moved away. There were tears in her eyes. When she sat down he knew he'd put off talking to her long enough. He needed her to know his plans. "I have to disappear for a while. It's best if I don't have any contact with you for awhile. Thomas set something up for me."

Thomas Miller was a friend of the family, not to mention cousin to his mom, and had been a very close friend of Coop's pop. He knew that he could trust Thomas as much as he had his own pop.

"I wondered if you were going to tell me or if I was just going to come in here one day and you'd be gone." She looked away, teary again. "What about your injuries? Will someone be able to care for you there?"

Coop nodded. "Yes. He said that there was a doctor who would see me whenever I needed and that the place was a fortress. He said there was no way anyone could get to me."

Wickett had been caught the same night that Coop had been shot. But that hadn't stopped the attempts on the chief's life. Nor had they been able to pin anything on the mayor. But if his approval rating was any indication, he wouldn't be living in the governor's mansion for much longer. That made Coop smile again.

"Will I be able to contact you?" she asked bringing him out of his thoughts. "See how you're doing at least? Or is that too much for a mother to ask?"

Coop laughed. It was the first laugh he'd had in almost two weeks. The pain shot through his belly, but it had been worth it. It was the first time he'd heard his mom laugh too. And it suited her to laugh.

"I'll get us both cell phones. They'll have to be disabled and the number can't be written down. Once we use it, you'll have to toss it." They'd done this before when he'd been undercover. "And I'll have Thomas send you whatever you need by the same route we used before."

He would give her a name. At the end of the call she would set up a post office box name for it under the guise of a vacationer and he'd send the phone there with only his new number programmed in. Mom had friends at the post office that helped her set this up and he was glad for it. In the meantime, he was going under the new identity of Payton Cooper. He'd been told stick to the truth as much as possible.

"I know how to use a disposable phone, young man. I didn't spend twenty-one years with another detective to have his son tell me how to keep someone I love safe. I'll expect weekly updates or else. You tell Thomas that I mean it or he'll have hell to pay too. And you don't want to know what the 'or else' means."

"Yes, ma'am. Weekly." Coop waited until she left to call Thomas. He was pretty sure his mom knew he was leaving today. She'd hugged him a few extra minutes before she'd left. Within an hour Coop left the private hospital and was on his way to the home of Doctor Cain Waite.

~Chapter 5~

Sin finally found her headphones. Why they were under her dish in the sink she didn't know. She'd had them yesterday when she ran and today someone had hidden them. She closed the door behind her before she remembered to check and see if she had a key.

She wasn't adapting well to living in the civilian world and she knew it. It was hard enough trying to simply not have someone telling her what to do every second of every waking hour, but all this free time was making her insane.

Stretching for twenty minutes, she set off at a slow pace to make her body wake up. At four in the morning she knew her sister wouldn't be awake, but some of the others on the street would be. She tried to avoid talking to them by wearing the headphones though there was nothing coming through them. But some people, people like Mrs. Carson down the street about halfway through her run, couldn't seem to get it that she didn't want to talk to her.

Sin hadn't spoken to many since she'd gotten back seven weeks ago. She didn't know what to say to them.

Mostly she tried to hide in the cabin, but her family, especially Alyssa, wouldn't take no for an answer. She frowned when she remembered the way they'd fought the other week.

"Damn it, it's just dinner. Get out of that house and come over or so help me, Sydney, I will come there and drag you here." Alyssa was getting frustrated and Sin could hear it in her voice. Well, damn it, so was she.

"What part of 'I'd rather be alone' did you not understand? I fucking like it here. Let me be."

She heard Alyssa count to ten, then to twenty before she said anything. "You're becoming a hermit. That can't be good for you. The doctor said you need to get out with—"

"I know what that fuck-tard said. He told me that I needed to acclimate myself to people better. What the fuck? I like it alone." Sin took a deep breath before she continued. "I'm thinking this isn't working out. I'm going to start looking for another place to stay. It's not your fault, I understand, but I can't keep having this argument with you every day."

"Please don't. Sin...please don't leave. Cain needs...I need you. Please don't. I'll...I'll leave you alone. I promise. If you have dinner with us tonight, I swear I won't bother you again."

And she hadn't, not in seventeen days. There had been texts from Cain, a note left on the door by Jazz, and even a card from Drew and Quinn, but nothing else. She wasn't sure what was going on, but she knew something was up. She was rounding the corner when she noticed Mrs. Carson's lights off.

Usually by the time Sin got here Mrs. Carson's entire house was aflame with lights. Today not even the porch light was on. It took her three minutes to get to the front of the house before she decided that it was none of her business. She was nearly a block away when she turned back.

"Fuck, fuck, fuck. This can't end well. I'm going to knock and she's going to be laying in wait for me. I just know it." Sin went up on the porch and looked in the window. "Mrs. Carson, its Sin Waite. Are you in there?"

Nothing. Not even her stupid little dog barked. She thought she heard something, but wasn't sure enough to break down the door yet. *Like I could.*

Moving around the house she saw the neighbor leaning against the porch rail smoking a cigarette. Sin started to ask him what he knew about Mrs. Carson, but he threw his butt at her and went inside his house.

Sin pulled out her cell phone when she heard something. Going up on the back porch, she leaned against the door and listened hard. Since she'd gotten hurt she couldn't hear anything in her right ear, but her left was fine. There! She'd heard it again, a mewing sound. When she heard the door open next door she ignored it and called the police.

"You need to step away from her house. She ain't home. I mean it, girl, you need to back on outta there now." Sin didn't turn, but did lower the phone from her ear when she heard someone answer.

"I'm going to call the police. I think I heard a noise from within Mrs. Adele Carson's house. My name is Sydney Waite."

"I don't give a good fuck who you are." The sound of a gun being racked shattered the otherwise silence of the morning. "I told you she ain't in there. Now you back on up and we'll pretend you was out for your run like you always are."

Sin decided she needed to change her route at that moment. She turned around slowly and could just make out the man with the smoke from earlier. "Fuck."

"You got that right. Now, I want you to drop your phone on the step and then come on down from there. You ain't got no reason to be making the call. I done told you she was gone and I'm…I'm protecting her house. Yeah, that's it, I'm protecting her house for her." His laughter made her skin crawl.

Sin started to say something when she saw what looked like Mrs. Carson's dog lying on the ground next to the neighbor's steps. He looked over where Sin was looking.

"He met with an accident." Again, the chilling laughter. "You ain't dropped that phone yet, girl. You deaf?"

Sin knew he was going to shoot her. And she'd had enough bullets taken out of her in one lifetime, thanks. She knew her chances of jumping out of range were slim to none, not with her bad leg, but she knew she could take him out. Gripping the phone, she threw it at him.

She had expected it to hit him; from the short distance of only about ten feet she'd throw hand grenades further. But what she didn't expect was it to hit him in the nose and to hit so hard that the gun discharged. She stood on the other step for a few seconds, shocked at the amount of blood that had erupted from his nose before she thought to rush him. Lucky for her, Mrs. Carson had a nice clothes line pole right next to the door and Sin scooped it up and wacked the man full on the head before he had a chance to recover.

He was dropping to the ground as she heard the police sirens. She didn't know if they were coming to her or somewhere up the street, but she did know that Mrs. Carson was in trouble. Picking up the shotgun she was careful not to touch the trigger as she walked back over to the house and slammed it against the glass at the back door, shattering it. She set the gun on the top step before she reached inside and opened the lock, cutting her arm open on the broken glass.

"Mrs. Carson? It's Sydney Waite. I'm in your house. If you're okay, I'm sorry about the broken glass. I'll pay for it when my next check comes." She rolled her eyes at herself. "I'm babbling because I'm bleeding and my leg hurts like a mother fu…it hurts."

She moved thorough the kitchen then in through the dining room. Still nothing. When she got to the living room, she found her.

Mrs. Carson was bleeding from her head and there was a nice gash on the side of her face too. Her eyes were wide as she looked up at Sin, so she fell to the floor next to her. Not graceful, but it was the best she could do.

"I called the Mp's…police. I hope." Sin reached out to take the gag out of her mouth, but Mrs. Carson flinched away. "I'm not going to hurt you. Let me get this out of your mouth."

When the gag was removed Mrs. Carson spoke. "He's coming back. He said that he was coming back. You have to hide."

Sin shook her head and just as she started to tell her that he wasn't coming back in here as long as she was here the front door burst open. Sin had about three seconds of bright light then nothing.

~~~

"This is the bedroom my sister is staying in. I told you she was very private, didn't I?" Coop nodded. Again. "She's recuperating herself. I don't know how she's going to react to you staying here, but I'm hoping she'll move in with Jazzy, our other sister, when she finds you here."

Coop didn't care. He just wanted to sit down and take a pain pill. His leg was throbbing and his head felt like a jackhammer was being used in it. He was nearly ready to tell Doctor Waite that he'd move to a hotel and call a taxi to take him when the man's cell phone went off.

"Waite… Yes, this is Cain Waite… Yes, my sist— what's happened to her?" Another long pause when the man sat down. All thoughts of his leg hurting flew out the window when Coop noticed how pale Cain looked.

"Cain," Coop asked as he hung up the phone. "What's wrong?"

"I have to go to the hospital. My sister…Sin, she's been…she hurt her leg and can't get home. I have to…I have to call Alyssa. I don't think…she told us to leave her alone. I knew she was running, but I didn't know where. She was in the worst part of town and she…I'm sorry. Can we do this some other time?"

"Let me go get her for you. Or take you. I can take you. You shouldn't be driving." Coop was leading Cain to his truck even as he realized he should just stay the hell out of this.

The ride to the hospital was long. Cain had made several calls on the way over and, in between those and telling Coop how to get to the hospital, Coop was able to gather a great deal about the man sitting next to him.

He was in love with his wife, for one—very much in love with her. He called her several times in the twenty minute drive and kept her informed of everything he did. He had an infant son named Connor and Captain Cait Grant was the local police and a good friend of the family. Of Sydney, aka Sin, he'd gathered much about her as well.

She was making her family pissed because she didn't want to be bothered with them. She'd just had a tragic accident that she was still being treated for and she was a royal pain in the ass. Coop had surmised that on his own when Cain had finally gotten to talk to her as they were pulling into a parking space marked Doctor Waite.

"Are you all right, Sin...Yes, I'm well aware that you're sick of hearing that question. If you'd let us see you once in a whi—don't take that tone with me, young...You learn that language overseas, girl?"

Yeah, Coop thought, a royal bitch.

The emergency room was a typical big city one. The sliding doors slid back quietly and the silence of the very early morning was broken by the overwhelming noise within the large, open room. Lots of cheap chairs and a few televisions turned on to cartoons or news. There was a reception desk right inside the door with several police milling about it and a well dressed woman who looked to be in her late forties to early fifties. She smiled when she saw Cain.

"You sister is pissed at you. I would suggest you stay out here until my men get her statement. You and she can take it up where you left off when you get her home."

"She was in the worst part of town at five in the morning and she didn't expect anything to happen to her. What was she thinking? She could just run the streets like a common fool and not get hurt?" Cain's voice rose with each word until he was shouting.

"Yeah, I can see why she's pissed. Alyssa said to keep you out here until she got here. She told me you need to take several deep breaths before...Cain, you're turning purple. I don't think that's a good color for you." Coop liked this woman, whoever she was.

Cain growled and it was all Coop could do not to laugh. He was hurting to do it too. When Cain looked over at him, the vein in his forehead throbbing, Coop lost it. The laughter that burst from his mouth was so unexpected that he surprised himself. When he glanced over at the woman, she too was laughing. Coop had to sit down before he fell or Cain knocked him down. That was how he met Mrs. Cain, laughing like a fool in a cheap plastic chair, wiping tears from his eyes.

"Well, I'm glad to see someone enjoys your temper tantrums. Cain, don't look at me like that. Here." Alyssa shoved a baby into Cain's arms. "Take your son. I'm Alyssa Waite, you must be Payton Cooper. Nice to meet you. Cait, what's going on?" And just like that, everyone was organized, had their assignments, and was doing everything Alyssa said.

"I'm going back to talk to Sin. You." Alyssa pointed at her husband. "Will sit right here until you can hold your temper. I will not have whatever you think you have to say to her bandied about this hospital, do I make myself clear?"

"I'm not a ten-year-old and I would very much appreciate it if you didn't treat me as one." Cain bounced his son on his knee as he spoke to his wife. "She was jogging in the middle of the night in a bad neighborhood. A man shot at her and she threw her knee out again. How does she expect us to take care of her when she does stupid shit like that?"

Alyssa didn't say anything for a full minute and when she did she sounded as pissed as her husband. "How old is Sin, Cain? Ten? Eleven? And where has she been for the past ten years? If you don't like being treated like a kid, then I would imagine she doesn't either. I'm going back to see her. When you can act like the adult that I know you are you can come back too."

When Alyssa went to the doors they opened and closed behind her while Cain and Coop sat on the chairs. Cain held his son up to his face and blew on his belly, making him laugh. Coop laughed with him.

"She's as worried as I am about Sin," Cain said after a second raspberry was blown on Connor's belly. "I almost lost her...my sister Sin. I almost lost her a few months back and I'm still...it's been hard thinking of her as the person lying in that hospital bed and this woman here. I still see her as my kid sister."

Coop nodded. He understood little sisters. "I have a sister too. Shaller Hall. She was married a few years back. Some dickweed that thought she should listen to him or his fists. She wouldn't listen to us when we tried to tell her. It took getting the shit beat out of her best friend before she decided being married to him wasn't such a smart move."

When a nurse came toward them she looked as if she was either pissed off or terrified out of her mind. She approached them with both caution and wariness.

"Captain Grant said for you to haul your ass on back there. Her words, not mine. She said if you don't want her to have to arrest your wife and sister you better move quick." She walked away, muttering under her breath about women with tempers and alcohol.

"Your wife brought alcohol to a hospital? I think I love your wife." Coop grinned when Cain glared. "You think if I'm ever in the hospital again she could smuggle me some in?"

"Might be sooner than you think. Stay away from my wife." Cain grinned. "You go in the room first, just in case they decide to throw something at me."

Even as far away as they were Coop could hear them as soon as they stepped through the door. Alyssa was laughing hysterically and Cait was talking. He could hear another person, a woman, and assumed it was the sister. When they opened the curtain and walked in Coop's breath caught.

"Holy mother of God. This is your baby sister?" He couldn't take his eyes from her. She was simply the most beautiful woman he'd ever seen. Even with the bloodied shirt and the black eye.

A short tumble of midnight black hair was curly and wild around her face. The bluest eyes he'd ever seen stared back at him from her oval face. Full lips, high cheekbones, and pert nose made him think of sultry nights, sweaty bodies, and sensual kisses. Coop could see a sprinkle of freckles dancing across her nose, brows arched and perfectly sculpted. Her neck was long and slender, smooth and muscled. He found himself wondering if he bit her there, just as her shoulder met her neck, would she taste as good as she looked? The tight running shirt molded and shaped to full, round breasts. Her nipples tightened while he watched and he felt his cock surge to life. And when she growled it was everything he could do not to join her in the bed and have his cock buried deep within what he knew were tight thighs and long legs.

"Payton Cooper, my sister, Sydney. Sin, this is Payton Cooper, I think he goes by Coop. He's your new roommate," Cain said.

~Chapter 6~

If the man didn't stop staring at her she was going to get up and punch him. He'd barely said three words since Cain made his announcement. Roommate, indeed. When pigs flew, that's when that was going to happen.

"Then what?" Cait asked. "After you checked the front door, what did you do? You said that he was on the back porch. How did you and Mr. Carmichael end up in the backyard together?"

"I went around to the back to see if I could find her. Mrs. Carson had been leaving her lights on since—does he have to be here? I mean, this is a statement, right? Should somebody like him be listening? What do we even know about him?" He grinned at her. "And wipe that smirk off your puss, buddy. I eat guys like you for breakfast."

"Sydney, I've told you twice, he's here visiting. He's a cop and I, for one, wouldn't mind a fresh set of eyes around here." Cait patted her hand like she was twelve. "Besides, shouldn't he get to know you firsthand? You are going to be living together."

"He is not going to be living with me. He is going to find other digs or I will. Cain, you said I could live there until I was ready to move on. Well, I'm not—"

"Oh get your panties out of a twist. I'm not going to cramp your style. I'm just hanging around until I can get my body back into shape." He didn't look to her like there was anything wrong with his body now. "Besides, you're just not my type. I like my women a whole lot less butch."

Sin nearly went after him, might have too if the doctor hadn't picked that moment to come into her area. She would deal with Mr. Cooper later.

"No concussion, which is good. I'm going to have Nurse Lear stitch up your brow and then you can go. It says here you don't want any drugs. I'm afraid you'll need to have at least a local to have—"

"No. Nothing. If she doesn't want to stitch it then I'll do it myself. But no drugs. And no tape either. I'm allergic." Sin looked over at Cain who was nodding. "He's my doctor. You have questions beyond what I can't answer then ask him."

"Miss Waite, I'm afraid I'm going to have to insist that you—"

"You can *insist* all you want. No drugs or no stitches. Up to you, doc. Either way, in an hour I'm outta here." Coop looked like he was going to say something, but seemed to change his mind when Cain stood up.

"I'll put them in," Cain said with a heavy sigh. "I might put a few in her mouth too while I'm at it. Finish up, Sin. When you need a ride home, call me. I'll come and get you."

When he left, the room was silent for several seconds. Coop thought for sure she would call him back and, when she didn't, he stood again.

"You're a piece of work, aren't you? Your brother nearly passed out when he heard you were hurt and what do you do? You treat him like shit because he was concerned about you." He started out of the curtain. "And I am living in the house. You can bunk with your sister if you want, but I'm staying in the house."

Probably not the best start to a live-in relationship. But Coop couldn't get the image of Cain nearly falling down out of his mind. Then the ungrateful bitch had acted like she was too good to be in his presence. Coop went out to the parking area and waited for Cain. There was no way he was going to be around Miss Waite any longer than necessary.

The ride back to Cain's office was quiet. He had left his wife there, telling her that he would meet her at the house later. He had two patients to see and she had a board meeting. Coop dropped him off and left without saying much more than thanks for the key. It took him less than twenty minutes to get his gear in the house and into one of the bedrooms. He didn't know which was Queenie's, but he was willing to bet it was the biggest room in the place.

Not that his room was shabby. The walls were a nice creamy wallpaper and the comforter and the pillows were a couple shades darker. The floors were a beautiful knotty pine and shone brightly from lots of care. He went to one of the three windows and opened it to let in the morning air. It overlooked the backyard and he could see someone had set up some sort of workout area. He wondered if Cain got to use it much when he turned away to start unpacking. The first thing he did was call his mom.

"Well, I'm here. Nice place. The people are great too. How are you holding up?"

"Your sister is here. She's met someone. Seems to think he's the right one. I don't know. I think she is marrying again because she's lonely. I told her to find one of those friends and not to get married." He heard her mumble something to someone then came back. "She said to tell you she misses you already."

Coop was still trying to wrap his head around his mother telling his sister to find a friend with benefits. And to use the benefits part. Coop sat down hard on the bed.

"Mom...Mom, would you like me to run a check on this guy? I can...please don't ever speak to me about sex again. I don't think...damn it, Mom, seriously?" Her laughter made him smile. "You are one sick woman, sick. So has Shaller really met someone or was that a joke too?"

"Yes. But it's nothing serious. He's a friend of that man...what is his name... Oh well, it'll come to me. Anyway, I'm glad you made it all right. Do you need anything?"

"No. I'm fine. Met my doctor today. Nice guy. His family is a bit off, but all right I guess." Well, with the exception of one, he thought.

They talked for a few more minutes and he gave her a name. He knew within the next day or so he'd have to go and get her a phone and mail it to her from Kelly Marcum. He was just laying down when he heard a car pull up then leave. Not bothering to get up, he waited for her to come into the house and blast him. When nothing happened after a bit he started to go and find her and couldn't make himself get up off the bed. He was drifting off when he thought of where he'd parked his car. He should probably have moved from in front of the garage.

It was late afternoon when he woke up. He'd been napping like this since he'd been shot. The doctor told him it was his body trying to tell him it needed rest and to let it have it. Coop didn't like it, but he always felt so much better afterwards that he started simply going to sleep when he felt tired.

The house was quiet when he got downstairs. There was no note on the table or anything written on the big chalkboard in the kitchen. He knew he had to get something to eat soon and wondered if Queenie even knew how to cook when she walked into the kitchen.

The jogging outfit and sheet lying across her in the hospital had hidden a great deal, he thought. Sydney was every bit of six feet tall and the heels she had on added an additional three inches to her already mouthwatering height. The little black dress she had on fit like it had been painted on her and her bare legs made him want to chew on something, like her legs.

Coop was a leg man. He loved the curve of a woman's calf, the turn of her ankle, and especially the tone of her thighs. Coop could see every inch of her legs and knew that Miss Waite had a very nice package. When he looked at her foot it was tapping a mile a minute. He took his time looking back up her body to her face.

"Enjoy the view? Maybe you should take pictures, that way when you're jerking off in the shower later you'll have an image to go with whatever fantasy you've dreamt up."

"No thanks. I won't forget this." He grabbed the counter when she leaned into the fridge. The view from this angle was just as wonderful, he thought. "You have a very nice ass, Miss Waite. Anyone ever tell you that?"

"Several hundred men no different than you. I don't shop for you. You see something in here you want, forget it. I've moved my stuff to the bottom shelf. And the right drawer is mine. The bottom shelf of the door is mine as well. I don't have anything in the cabinets so they're all yours." She poured herself a glass of amber liquid. "I drink tea, no sugar, no ice. You drink it and don't replace it, I'll castrate you. Any questions?"

He was still thinking of her bending over every time she opened the fridge and almost forgot to breathe. He decided that he'd make it a point to be in the kitchen when she was. He had plenty of questions for her, though. Did she like it hard and fast, or slow and easy? Could he take her against the table or would she sit on his cock in one of the chairs and ride him until they were both screaming? Would she suck his cock and could he please taste her—

"Mr. Cooper, are you all right?"

He nodded. It was that or moan. He was going to be living with the ice goddess and he was going to die of a perpetual hard-on. The knock at the front door had him nearly drawing his gun.

She breezed out of the kitchen door and Coop leaned against the counter. When he heard the man's voice he adjusted his cock again and moved into the living room where some guy was helping her on with her wrap and looking down the front of her dress while he stood behind her.

"Hello. I'm Payton Cooper. And you would be?"

Sydney stood in front of his outstretched hand. "None of your business. We have to live together, but we are far from going to be friendly." She turned to the man and her smile to him took his breath away. "If you're ready, we can go."

Coop stood there for several seconds then, grabbing up the newspaper on the end table next to the door, he took a pen from the little vase near the phone and wrote down the license plate number of Mr. BMW. He had no idea why he cared, but he tore off the number of the out of state plate and stuck it in his wallet. Might be useful to pin her murder on the guy if she continued to drive him insane.

~~~

Sin hated dating. She'd been out on three with Rick...sorry, Richard Conway and she decided that this was the last one. Sure, he was funny if you were ten. He was good-looking, she supposed. Not as good-looking a Coop was, but a woman couldn't be too choosey.

Coop looked like a man that could put on a tux and look great, or nothing at all and look better. Sin reached out and adjusted the vent to blow in her face. Christ. This was not good.

She decided it was the beard. Not a beard, but a goatee the same warm brown as his hair. The only men she'd been around for ten years were clean shaven. Rules like that were never fucked with in the Army. Sin found herself wanting to brush her lips across his to see if it was soft or bristled. She was betting soft.

Then there were his eyes. Men shouldn't be allowed to have eyes the color of solferino; the light purple color was suited more to amethyst or even sapphires, but not eyes. His were beautiful and when he was pissed…which now that she thought of it was most of the time, they darkened. Adjusting the fan again, this time turning up the speed, she thought about how they looked when he was staring at her in the kitchen. Lust and more. Sin would bet that Payton could satisfy without even trying. She would even go so far as to—

"Are you listening to me? I swear I could have had an accident for all the attention you were paying." Sin glanced over at what's his name. "Is it because of what happened today?"

She tried to remember what had happened today. Her body was hot, her pussy was wet, and she needed to… "You mean with Mrs. Carson? Oh no…yes, that's it. I was so worried about her. The doctor said she was going to be fine in a few days."

"Can you tell me what happened? I mean, if you're up to it. I know things like that can upset women and make them nervous."

Sin glanced at him again. He couldn't be serious. She'd spent the last ten years in the service and she'd seen more death and even caused a few of her own to last several lifetimes.

Shrugging and not really caring about his ego, she answered. "Nah, didn't bother me. I've seen worse. Much worse. There was this time when the seven of us had to go into a castle in Da Nang, a South Central Coast of Vietnam, and take out this guy who had decided he was going to rule. We snuck in through the side door where the servants would enter and killed nineteen of his guard before we even made it to his bedroom. There were seven more just—"

"You're kidding, right? The war in Vietnam ended before we were even born. There is no...you're pulling my leg." He laughed. "You have a very strange sense of humor, Valeria."

She looked at him sharply. "My name is Sydney or Sin. Actually, I prefer Sin if you don't mind. How did you find out my middle name anyway?"

He laughed again. "But Sydney is so common and Sin...well, that just won't do. Your middle name...well, my mommy thought it would be a good idea to have you investigated before it got too serious. You know, the name Conway can't be attached to just anyone. We have a great deal of pride in our heritage."

Sin looked out the front of the car. Her mood went from lusty to pissy in two mikes...minutes. She needed to remember the civilian way the world spoke. "Heritage, huh? I don't suppose it hurts that my brother is married to a Howard either, does it?"

"No. Actually, that was the deciding factor for Mommy. She said that even though she thought that Alyssa married beneath her station she did have that nasty business with her mother being murdered by her own son to worry about more."

Sin wanted to laugh, but she was afraid he'd not laugh with her. He called his mother "Mommy?" She couldn't help it, she snorted. The look he gave her did make her laugh.

Dinner was a disaster and she was glad to be going home. There was no other way to describe it. He'd been telling her of her future attached to his for over an hour and all she wanted to do was to tell him to fuck off. But she thought about the dates before him, the ones where she wished she'd worn a Chastity Belt and carried a stun gun. She'd gone home from those with her virginity barely intact—if she had been a virgin.

The other two times they'd gone out, they'd gone to a gallery opening the first time, which wasn't too bad. She enjoyed meeting the artist and his wife seemed like a nice person. It wasn't until she was looking at one of his pieces alone that Byron came up behind her and spoke.

"I know you. Well, I used to know you. You're Cain's little sister, the one who was in the news recently." She didn't turn around. "They said you were a hero."

"Yeah, that's me. Some hero I turned out to be." She turned then and looked at him. "Is my pedigree not good enough to be in your gallery, Mr. Grant? Or can I stay because Alyssa is my sister-in-law?" As soon as the words left her mouth she'd been sorry. She'd had no right to take her bad mood out on him. But before she could tell him she was sorry he threw back his head and laughed.

"Yeah, Taylor said that Ricky was a pain in your ass. No, Miss Waite, don't go. Shall we start over?" He walked closer to her and held out his hand. "Hello, I'm Bryon Grant. I'm the potter. I believe we knew each other a long time ago."

This time she laughed. "Sin Waite at your service. Ricky? I'm sure his mommy would not appreciate that slang term."

They had met twice more since then, Byron and his really nice wife Taylor, for lunch and once for dinner. In fact, Taylor had helped her pick out this dress.

The second time had been to a function. She wasn't sure what the function had been, but it involved her hanging on his arm and biting her tongue a great deal. The only redeeming thing was that Byron, Taylor, and his brother Jamie and his wife Dane had been there.

They pulled up in front the house and she started to open the door. He hated when she did that. He wanted to walk all the way around the car, open her door for her, and hand her out. Hand her out like she was some royalty or something. Fucking retard. If he tried to kiss her tonight she was going to give him a quick jab to the nuts and then step over his body and into the house. Her head hurt and she was tired. And he kissed like she thought a frog might kiss.

Having enough, she waited until he was in front of the car then opened the door herself and got out. He huffed at her. And she wasn't sure, but she thought he might have stomped his foot.

"Valeria, I have asked you repeatedly to wait for me to come around. A gentleman opens the door for his date."

"Sorry. But I have to pee. You drive carefully home." She might have made it too if she hadn't forgotten to get her key out. She hadn't locked a door in so long she always forgot the key.

"Valeria, aren't you going to invite me in? It's been such a lovely evening that I thought maybe you and I could sit in front of the fireplace and talk."

Inspiration hit. "You'll have to split wood for that. Oh, I love that. You can find the axe in the back on the wood pile. I think there are some small enough pieces in here that I can get one started. But no big stuff. You do that, I'll pee and then work on the fire."

"You mean for me to cut wood? Like...like a commoner? Oh no, why don't you go in and ask that man, the one with the beefy arms, to do it? I can start the kindle, he can tote the wood inside for us then leave. That's a much better plan."

She looked at him with wide eyes. This guy wasn't for real; there was no way he could be. "You want me to go and wake up Co...Mr. Cooper and have him cut us some wood for you to sit on the couch with me and talk? You're certifiable. I'm going in now. You go home before I have to hurt you."

She didn't even wait for him to answer, but shoved the key into the lock and opened it. With a quick, "night," she shut the door in his face.

"Fuck-tard. He didn't even ask me what happened to my eye." She was nearly to the kitchen when she realized she was too tired to mess with a glass of tea and turned to go to the basement. She was settled into her cot seconds after checking the room for unfriendlies. It was a habit she'd gotten into and she had yet to break it. Closing her eyes, she wasn't sure she wanted to.

~Chapter 7~

She was in the kitchen when he got up. Coop watched her from the doorway for a minute as she bent over to look into the refrigerator twice before she turned and looked at him. Today she was dressed in a royal blue running shirt and bright yellow bike shorts. What he wouldn't give to be her seat. Sitting down quickly he hoped she hadn't noticed that he was stiff as a board, and he didn't mean his leg.

"Where you off to at..." He glanced at his watch. "Fuck. Four in the morning?" He had never been up this early in his life unless it was before he had gotten to bed. "You can't possibly be going running again. I thought your brother told you to stay off that knee for a few days."

"And I told you to stay out of my way. I'm a grown woman and, believe it or not, I don't have to listen to my brother anymore. Hell, I never listened to him when I—"

"I'm going with you." He might have laughed at the expression on her face if he wasn't so sure she'd hurt him. "I need to start exercising my leg again. Cain told me I should start trying to move it more."

Cain had actually told him to start out slow and move up to running, but for reasons he didn't want to think about, letting Sydney go out again on her own bothered him. He stood up and told her to wait. He wanted to go and get his shoes. With as much power as he could he left the kitchen without limping...too much.

When he got back she was just pulling on her sweatshirt. "I must be stupid. Here I am waiting like an idiot for some halfwit to go with me on a run when he can barely walk. Stay here, Mr. Cooper. I want to get going and I'm not waiting on you."

"I'm ready." When she stood there staring at him he was sure she was going to refuse, but she simply went out the door and to the backyard to the brightly lit equipment.

Watching a woman stretch in the morning was another of Coop's favorite things. Especially naked stretching after spending the entire night making love and she got up to go to the bathroom. Women had the most amazing bodies. They had muscles that moved all sorts of delightful parts. Breasts bounced, nipples peaked and hardened. Coop loved women. But watching Sydney stretch on the equipment before her run nearly killed him.

He stood watching her for several minutes. He knew she was aware of him; she'd be hard pressed not to be. Whenever she turned around to glare at him, he made sure there was no drool on his chin when she looked back to what she was doing. He was just glad that he'd opted for loose gym pants. But he was reasonably sure if she kept this up these would be much too small as well. He decided to get going and try to ignore her. *Yeah right!*

Leaning on the bar, he started doing some slow stretches. His leg already ached and he wasn't sure how far she usually ran, but if they went further than the end of the drive he was going to die.

"How long ago were you hurt?"

He glanced at her and saw that she was looking at his leg. It was obviously less toned than the other. "Just shy of six weeks." He lifted his shirt. "This one caused the most damage. I had to change my diet and my way of moving for this."

The bullet had entered his small bowel. Had his mother not shown up when she had he'd be eating and shitting in a bag permanently attached to him. As it was, he'd lost a good portion of his gut along with a part of his liver.

She looked at him, not saying anything, and Coop thought he'd bothered her. When she stood up and lifted her own shirt it took him several deep breaths before he could speak.

"They were more concerned with putting me back together than they were making it pretty. I have one more on my head, but my hair pretty much covers it."

They were bullet holes, three…no, four of them. They were pink, not as pink as his, but recent. He stepped forward and started to lay his hand on her when she stepped back. He looked down at her face.

"I can't…I can't touch them yet. I can't even look at them. I get dressed in the dark and try my best to pretend they're not there." Her voice was tight and low, full of emotion he couldn't fathom. "They told me I can have them fixed later, but…I don't think I can do…"

"How? When?" He'd heard she'd been hurt a few months ago, but he'd not known how or how badly.

She lowered her shirt and turned her back to him. "Seventeen months. I have steel rods in both legs. It's why I run. If I don't then I get stiff and can't walk. The service...Army. I was there for ten...we can walk today. I'm sort of sore because of the shoes I wore last night. If you're finished, we can start."

She didn't wait for him, but turned and walked away. Coop moved after her and, once he was beside her, she slowed her pace and put a set of earphones in her ears. Conversation over for now, he guessed. But he wanted...no, he needed more information than this. Someone had tried to kill her and had nearly succeeded. And Payton Riley Cooperider felt like a total ass.

People seemed to know her, but for the most part she just waved. When they came to a crosswalk or a stop sign she would stretch again. He did as well. He wasn't so far gone in lust that he couldn't recognize that she was slowing her pace for him, nor did he not notice the men who were out on their porches drinking their coffee when they went by so early in the morning. He had been glaring at one particular man when Sydney spoke.

"They don't care. All they see is a pair of tits and a firm ass. Could be that he's looking at you anyway." She said it so seriously that he had to stop to stare at her. She actually believed that men were only looking at her because of her boobs?

When she turned to look at him she smiled and he just had to ask. "You don't believe that, do you? That men only think you're beautiful because of how you're shaped?"

"What did you see the first time you saw me? It was my tits, I bet. You can't lie to me. I've been hanging around men for too long to not know a thing or two about the way they think."

Coop flushed. It was. "*No*! Your black eye. I saw it first." She snorted. "Okay, then, your boobs. You are such a tiny thing I guess I was amazed you could carry them around. And for the record, could you please stop calling them tits? I'd think, as a woman, you'd find that word—"

She cupped her breasts and lifted them up. Christ, he nearly tripped over his own tongue. "They are just fatty tissue that just happen to have a very high arousal zone in them. Nothing more. Oh, and milk glands."

"Sydney, you can't...you shouldn't do that to a man. You could hurt me, us. You could hurt us."

She snorted again. "Men and sex. Big deal. You know if you had an itch and scratched it, it would be okay. Other men would pound on their chests with you. They would have a party in your honor. If I had the same itch women would go out of their way to scorn me and treat me like I have some sort of mental health problems."

He knew he was going to regret asking. He knew it as soon as the question formed in his head, but he had to know. He needed to know. "Do you have an itch, Sydney?"

She stared at him for long moments then simply put her headphones back in and started walking back toward the way they had come.

"It doesn't matter anymore. I won't have sex with anyone again because of the scars. Men, like you were, will be appalled." She glanced back at him again. "I'm going to run back the rest of the way. I'll catch you later."

He watched her take off. She was nearly two blocks away before he moved to follow. He didn't just feel like an ass now, he felt his heart crush under the weight of what he'd done.

~~~

It had been three days since she'd seen Mr. Cooper. She'd done well to avoid him and now he was in the kitchen when she was about to go out. She had a date with Taylor and Dane. They were going to have a girl's night out. Sin was dressed in her new dress her sister Grace Anne had sent her for her birthday. She was twenty-eight today.

"There's mail for you. I didn't know which room you were in so I just hoped you'd see it here. Where are you sleeping anyway?"

She let out a slow breath, glad he wasn't going to bring up their conversation from the other day. "Basement. There are a couple of rooms down there. I'm using one as a weight room and the other as a bedroom." She picked up the first envelope and knew it was from her sister Jazzy. "The weight equipment is Cain's. He's letting me use it. If you want to use it, too, just wipe it down when you're done."

The card was bright and cheery and she had enclosed a gift certificate to her favorite lotion shop. She picked up the second card. It was from Quinn and Drew. There was the usual happy birthday and a "we miss you very much" penned inside.

The third card was from her sister Lilliane. There was a nice and very long note inside that said she missed her, but it was the last that made her smile.

"As identical twins I feel I must tell you that you need to get laid. I can feel your needs all the way here. If you don't do the nasty with the first person you see—I don't even care which sex at this point—I will be forced to do it for you. I love you, baby sis. Lizzy"

She was still laughing when she looked up at him. "What?"

"I don't think I've ever seen you laugh before. It's very beautiful on you. You should do it more often."

Sin flushed, she could even feel her cheeks heat. "It's my birthday and my family sent me cards. My sister, Lillianne, or Lizzy, is my twin and she said…she told me something personal and it made me laugh, that's all. I should go." She was gathering up her things to leave when he tapped her on the shoulder.

She turned to him slowly, afraid of what he might say to ruin her good mood. Or better yet, how she would take whatever he said to ruin her mood. Instead, he cupped her face and brought it to his.

"Happy Birthday." The kiss, like his words, was soft and gentle. When he pulled back and looked at her she wasn't sure what to say and was glad she didn't because he pulled her back and kissed her again. This one had more heat, more mouth, and a great deal more touching.

He pulled her body to his, flush against him. She could feel every muscle, every contour, and every bit of his erection against her. When he shifted his head and deepened the kiss Sin moaned and wrapped her free hand into his shirt. She needed to hang onto something or fall. When he pulled away and took a step back she was as close to begging a man to take her as she'd ever been. Need coiled not only in her belly, but in every cell of her, every pore, even her hair seemed to need him But when he took another step back she reached behind her for the door knob and twisted it open. She was out the door and in her car before she could say something incredibly stupid like, "why did you stop? Take me, big boy." Sin was pulling into the restaurant parking lot when she realized she must have looked stupid anyway and laid her head on the steering wheel.

"Could this get any worse? Do you think maybe, I don't know, you could go one whole day without making an utter fool of yourself?" She got out of the car. "I'm guessing not," she said as she noticed the keys still in the ignition and the tab down in the locked position on the door.

Dinner was fun. She was extremely glad she'd decided to go. They had just ordered when Dane turned to her with a smile.

"So, how was it? Was it as good as you look like it was?" Sin looked at her, confused. "The kiss. It was the first time he kissed you, right?"

"Kiss? Who kissed you? Oh my God, that guy...Coop? He kissed you? Way awesome. Go give it up, girl. Was it good or what? I bet he's a Dom too. I can tell. Byron said so too." Taylor crunched a breadstick as she finished. "I'll make sure you guys have an invite to the club. It's a lot of fun and you can have all the freebies you want. I'll tell Byron to set it up for you."

"Whoa, girl, I'm not sleeping with…Dom? Byron is a…? Then you're his…? Well, fuck me." Sin just looked at both women as they burst out laughing.

"No, dear, that's for Coop to do. And yes, I'm Bryon's sub to his Dom. We actually met that way. He owns and operates several clubs called Tightly Bound. Have you heard of them?"

Sin picked up her glass of tea and drained it. "No. But I don't do that. I mean, it's okay and all, but Coop, Mr. Cooper, and I aren't lovers. He just kissed me for my birthday."

"It's your birthday? Why didn't you say something? We could have had a big party for you. I love throwing parties. You and Coop will have to come to…what is it, dear? What's wrong?" Dane patted her on the arm. "Ah, those. Let me tell you firsthand, men who love you don't notice the scars. They just love you."

"You're scary, you know that? Besides, I'm a tad too old for parties. I was really surprised when Gracie sent me this dress. She said it's one of hers. I love it. Of course it would fit because we're sisters and all, but…now what did I say?"

"You're related to Grace Anne? Grace Anne the designer? Holy shit. You have to let me meet her. I love her things. I have two of her dresses in my closest at home." Taylor blushed. "I know, I'm gushing, but since I've married Byron I find I love sexy things against my skin. He does too."

Sin looked at both the women. She simply couldn't help it, she starting laughing. "When we were kids Gracie would dress up our neighbor's cat. She told me that she was going to be famous someday and that women all over the world would be talking about her dresses over champagne and carrots. We didn't have a clue what caviar was so she said carrots. You have to tell her." Sin dug out her phone and dialed. "She'll love that you love her stuff and all."

They spent the next twenty minutes with Gracie on speaker phone then finished their dinner. Sin couldn't remember a more enjoyable night, especially on her birthday. When they departed they had decided to make this a weekly thing and to invite Margaret Parker, the older women's mother-in-law, and the other girls, Morgan, Ronnie, and Cait—the other Grant women.

She drove home after calling the car service to get her keys unlocked from the car, knowing she had made some good friends, women friends, something she didn't seem to have any of. Going into the house she went to the basement without checking the house out. She didn't have the energy to deal with Mr. Cooper and his kiss right now. After checking for unfriendlies she went to her cot, curled into a tight ball, and fell asleep. She had a doctor's appointment late tomorrow and wanted to get in a good run before then.

~Chapter 8~

Coop was in the kitchen when she came in. When she stopped suddenly and stared at him and the gift on the table he knew she'd not ignored it like he'd thought, but had simply not seen it. He was both relieved and annoyed. And he couldn't figure out either emotion.

"You have a party to go to this morning, Mr. Cooper? Seems a bit of an odd time, but I don't know that much about things in the States anymore." She opened the refrigerator and leaned down to get her tea.

"Sydney, I've had my tongue down your throat and your body pressed intimately against mine. Do you think you can dispense with the 'Mr.' part and call me Coop, or even by my first name Payton? The gift is for you. I'm sorry, I didn't know it was your birthday." Coop wanted to pull her body close to his again and tangle with her mouth in the worst way. "Did you have a nice time last night?"

She sat across from him and played with the ribbon on the package without looking at him. "When I was seven years old my father got me a gift. It was the only one I ever received from him. It was even wrapped. My sister

Lizzy, my twin, got one as well." She looked up at him then. "It was a drill. Not a cheap one, but one that costs a small fortune today. Lizzy got a tool box. This is the first present that I've ever received that was wrapped since then."

"Sydney, I'm sorry, honey. I didn't know. Here, let me take this off." When he reached for it, she grabbed his hand.

"Don't. I'm sorry. I don't…I have no idea why I told you that. I hadn't…would you mind if I didn't open it right now? I want to go on a run and I'm not in a place where I can appreciate this right now." She stood up and looked down at him. "You can't kiss me anymore either. It was really nice, great, but Richard asked me to marry him and I said yes."

"Why? You don't love him. Actually, I thought he was gay when I sort of met him the other week." Coop stood up and she backed up. He moved toward her again.

"He is. I mean, no. He is, but he doesn't want his mommy to—could you please back up? Why are you forever trying to back me into things? It's very annoying." She bumped against the refrigerator and pressed her hands against his chest. "You have to back off. Now, Mr. Cooper."

"I do it so I can do this." He cupped the back of her head and pulled her mouth to his.

There was no resistance even though he expected it. Nor did she hesitate in opening beneath him. Her mouth was cool from the tea, but warmed immediately under his tongue. She tasted of mint and of her. He wanted her in the most carnal sense. Beneath him, over him, around him, any of those ways, all of them. Sliding his hand up her ribs he felt her breath catch and he brushed his hand over the tip of her breast; her nipple rubbed against his palm. When she arched into his hand he reached down and pulled her shirt up. He needed to taste her flesh and could think of nothing but that. When her lacy, covered breast was exposed he pulled his mouth from hers and laved the black lace with his tongue then bit.

"Payton, please." He didn't care what she wanted, he was willing to give it to her. Moving the bra down with his thumb he took her nipple into his mouth and suckled. Her fingers at the back of his head made his cock burn with need. Rocking into her, they both moaned and he reached between her legs and felt her heat.

The phone ringing in her pocket made her stiffen. He wanted to scream out his frustration when he felt her pulling back both mentally and physically. He let go of her nipple, but went back for another quick nip and was happy when she tightened her fingers in his hair once more before she let him go.

She stood there breathing hard as she pushed at his chest. He stepped back again, but didn't let her go. He couldn't. Not yet at any rate. He was afraid if he did, he'd fall on his face. While he watched she adjusted her bra back up and pulled her shirt down.

"We can't do this. Never. Do you understand me? I'm going to marry Richard because he won't...you want too much. More than I can give you."

"How do you know what I want from you is more than you're willing to give me? How do you know what I can give you isn't just what you want?" He pulled her in for another kiss. She responded as she had before. "You want me as much as I want you, Sydney. Are you willing to settle for Richard because he's safe?"

"Yes." She stepped to the side and out of his arms. "Yes, I am. I have to go." She was out the door before he could stop her.

Coop sat in the chair and looked around the kitchen. What the hell had just happened? Every time he thought he understood her or had a handle on her, she would bring something else out on the table. He was going nuts, that was it. Nutty as a fruitcake. He needed to burn off some of this energy. Going to the basement door he decided to take her up on her offer to use the equipment.

The equipment was state of the art. There was everything anyone could ever hope to find in an expensive gym. There was a weight bench and a NordicTrack, an elliptical and a rower. In the corner there were weight, squat, and step machines. He opened the other door, looked in, and had to lean against the wall for support.

Sydney had made the smallish room into her bedroom. There was an army cot along with a sleeping bag on it. She had a pillow and a table that he'd seen the match for in the living room. On it was a lamp, book, and a canteen. In the corner was a dorm-sized refrigerator and a hotplate on top of it. The only window had been blacked out with a heavy, woolen-looking blanket. Her clothes were folded neatly and lying on a duffel bag, and her shoes, both civilian and service, were polished and set near the bag. With all the bedrooms in this house she felt the most comfortable in her own version of army life. Coop went out to the equipment and started to work out. He tried not to think of the woman who lived here with him.

~~~

"I don't care what you have to do to find him, I want that fucker found. He is fucking with my livelihood and I want him dead." Carl began pacing the floor. "He's been gone now almost two months and not a word from anyone."

"It's only been about seven weeks, sir, not two months." The man speaking had no idea when to shut up, apparently. "I think he was picked up by his—"

Carl shot him in the head. There was going to be a mess, but he was too far gone right now to give a good flying fuck about that. That's what cleaning services were for. He put his gun away and turned to the other two men standing there.

"Either one of you want to correct me on how long that cock sucker has been gone." They both shook their heads no. "Good. Moving on. He did have a point. Did his mother stash him somewhere and he's out there just waiting or did he die and no one has informed me yet?"

One of the two idiots cleared his throat before speaking. "I don't believe he's dead, sir. If he is, his family sure isn't taking it all that hard. Unless they hated him as much as you do. Could be that."

"No, he was a momma's boy, pure and simple. If he were dead I'm sure she'd have some fucking black arm band on every cop in the city by now. I need to move and I can't move until this trial is over. And it won't be over to my satisfaction until Cooperider is dead."

He sat down at the desk. There were all sorts of photos spread everywhere on it and nothing of value. He'd had the family followed since he'd been arrested and Carl was no closer to finding his accuser than he'd been that night. There were pictures of his mother going to meetings, to dinners. There were pictures of his sister going with her on some, but mostly Mrs. Cooperider with her bevy of bodyguards. He raked his hand across the entire mess and threw them to the floor.

"How can one near death man just disappear like that? He would have had to go to the hospital somewhere. He had a gut shot that would have required surgery. I know, I put that one there myself. This was planned out and planned." He closed his eyes. "How did whoever picked him up know where to find him? And better yet, how did the chief find out?"

"Maybe he used his own phone to text someone? You were listening in, right? Wouldn't take much to text, say…the chief then have him bring somebody in to save him." Carl looked at the man who'd just figured out what he'd been working on for weeks. "I mean, that's what I'd do."

Carl toyed with the idea of shooting his bastard too, but glanced over at the bloody mess already staining his carpet and the chair he'd been standing near. He saw the two men start to move and decided that for now they would both live. For now. He stood up again and took out his gun. He smiled to himself when they both backed up a step.

"I've thought of that too. But who would he trust besides the chief? His list of buddies in the department is less than zero, I made sure of that. Who else then?" Carl wasn't expecting an answer and wasn't surprised when he didn't get one. "His sister, mother? Surely he wouldn't bring his family into a hostile place to save his pansy ass, would he?"

"My mom would be the last person I'd trust, but by all accounts this feller has a good relationship with his. Could be she pulled some strings and had her baby boy put on ice somewhere outta state." Carl looked at the other man. "She wasn't from around here, right?"

Carl got up and got the file. "No, she was from Ohio. Do we know anyone in Ohio who could do some searching? Or better yet, you go. I need someone I can trust."

"What about me? I can help him." The second guy actually raised his hand. "I'm pretty good with searching."

Carl glanced at the other man. He gave a small shake of his head. Carl nearly laughed out loud. He didn't know any of their names, but he thought he might like this guy. "No, I have something else you can do. *After* you get rid of this body." He looked at the smarter one. "What's your name anyway?"

"Shipley, Roger Shipley."

"Well, Shipley, you can look up someone else for me while you're doing some searching in Ohio. I have a wife there that I'd like to know the whereabouts of. Her name is Quinn Waite. She was supposed to have married some dick a few months back, but don't know if that panned out. See what you can find out about her and there's a bonus in this for you." Carl took out his wallet and gave Shipley five grand. "Use this to get the balls rolling on either of those assignments. Keep me updated on anything you find. Use my personal number."

Shipley nodded as he took the money. He simply opened his own wallet and slipped the cash inside. After a few more instructions Shipley left. Carl was just going out the door himself when the idiot spoke up.

"How do I get rid of this body, Mr. Wickett? There anyone in particular I can call?" Carl was tempted once again to shoot him, but didn't. The mess wouldn't get cleaned up and he'd have two bodies to get rid of instead of just the one.

"I don't give a good fuck, it just had better be gone when I return. And make sure you get this carpet cleaned too. I can't have all this blood messing up my décor."

Carl thought he might hurt himself thinking about the expression on the guy's face when he'd told him about the décor. He was still laughing when he went to dinner with the mayor, in his home no less.

~Chapter 9~

Sin brushed angrily at the tears. *Fat lot of good they'll do you*, she thought viciously. She looked down at the gun in her hand. But this…this would solve a great deal.

"You going hunting tonight, Sydney? Seems kinda late, don't you think? And that isn't a hunting type of weapon anyway."

Coop's voice startled her. She hadn't even realized she'd been followed, she'd been so upset. She dropped the gun back down and behind her.

"Go back in the house. This…I have some things to work out and I do that better when I'm alone. I have things under control now."

She nearly screamed when, instead of turning to go back, he took two steps toward her. Damn it, she needed him gone, not right here.

"I was thinking that too. That you have things under control…or so you think you do. What's going on? Sometimes talking it over with someone can make things less overwhelming." He took another step toward her. "But then talking is highly overrated too."

"That's what I was thinking. You go away. I don't want to talk to you. I mean it. Just go back…stop walking toward me, damn it." Coop had taken two more steps and now he was within five feet of her.

"It's a full moon, did you notice? And here I am with a lovely woman…makes a man have cravings, wants, desires. You have desires, Sydney?" His voice was smooth, calm.

She brushed at the tears and took several deep breaths to calm herself. He would never leave if he saw how upset she was.

"Yes, Payton. It's a lovely night. I have desires…a desire to be alone for a bit. Could you just…just go back in the house and leave me to it?" Her voice cracked and sounded watery even to her. Sin hated herself and him at that moment.

"You didn't answer the question. You going hunting?" Another step brought him so close she could reach out and touch him. "You won't do a very good job with a handgun. Why don't you give it over and let me take it inside?"

She raised the gun to his chest, her temper snapped tight.

"You don't want to do that, Sydney. Shooting an innocent man isn't your style."

"How do you fucking know what my style is? For all you know I could be a killer hiding out here and I've lured you out here to murder you too." She waved the gun at him. "Go. Into. The fucking. House. Please?" She wanted to scream at him when he stepped closer, the gun touching his chest. Lifting the gun straight up, she fired. She expected him to tackle her, try to take the gun, but he let her put it back to his chest. "What is wrong with you? Are you nuts?" Sin felt the tears threaten again. "Go away. Please, I'm begging you. Go into the house and leave me be."

He ran his finger down her cheek as they stood there. "You didn't ask me what my desires were. I have one, a powerful one, truth be told. I've had it since the first time I saw you." He gently laid his hand over her wrist. "I've a desire to taste your mouth again. To see if it tastes as delicious as it did."

"Don't. Please don't do this. It's too late, too late for everything. Go into the house. You can just tell them you didn't know." She wasn't sure how he'd known what she was going to do, but she wasn't going to pretend it wasn't going to happen just because he did.

With his free hand he slowly cupped her neck and then brought her to his mouth. "No, you don't want to be alone, Sydney. Trust me."

The kiss was breathtakingly gentle. A simple brush of his mouth over hers. He didn't touch her anywhere else but her neck and her mouth, but the overwhelming power of that nearly made her knees buckle. Neither did he take the gun from her, she realized, but only touched the wrist that held it. When he raised his head she could see the moonlight reflecting back at her and she could see that his eyes had darkened with something.

"Do you want children, Payton?" Her voice was a mere whisper, but he seemed to hear her.

"Yes. Yes, I do. Lots of them with dark hair the color of midnight skies and eyes the color of summer days. You have children, Sydney?"

Sin laid her head on his chest, too tired to...too exhausted to fight anymore. Especially him. "No. No children." Never for her, never any children like the ones in her family. They'd taken that, all of that, from her.

"Then what's this about? Why are you out here in the middle of the night with a gun in your hand? Target practice? Maybe you thought you heard something that frightened you."

She started laughing and stopped when she realized how insane it sounded. "I highly doubt that. Very little frightens me, Cooper. I want you to go away and leave me be. Whatever you think you know, you're wrong."

He stared at her for a full minute. Then he brushed away another tear with his thumb before answering her. "Are you meeting a lover perhaps?" He shifted closer to her and she felt his erection. "Maybe you hoped to lure me out here to have your evil way with me. I'll tell you right now, I'm not going to be much of a challenge. You say *get naked,* and I'm right there with you."

This kiss was different, still gentle, but more. When his tongue touched her lips, she opened for him gave him her mouth. Another shift of his body brought his cock into her soft folds and a moan from him. They lined up perfectly, their bodies fit as one. When he pulled back slightly, she whimpered.

"Sydney, I need you to decide which steel you want to hold onto. I ache for your hand on me, love. Drop the one in your hand so I don't have to be jealous of it."

Confused for a second, she remembered the gun in her hand. He hadn't taken it from her. He hadn't touched it at all. But this was a test, a test only she could take and she didn't know what to do.

If she didn't drop the gun she knew he wouldn't walk away, but he would try and take it from her. That she knew. She wasn't sure he could, but he would try. She also knew that one if not both of them would be hurt if he did. And not just physically. If she dropped it, then what?

Was she saying she would try later? Or was this admitting she'd been wrong contemplating shooting herself in the first place? Did she even want to anymore?

"I can't imagine what you might be feeling right now. I do know that I would never have pegged you as a coward. A woman as full of spit and vinegar as you taking your own life rather than facing what ifs and could have beens."

His voice touched something inside of her. "Let me go." He did so immediately. "You don't know what you're talking about. You have no idea what those men…what they did to me. You've no—"

"No one does. You've got your entire family walking around on egg shells, too afraid to ask you how you're feeling to try and ask you the important questions. What did they do to you, Sydney? We all know they beat you, shot you. But as far as I can tell that's about all they did to you physically. What did they do to fuck with your head that has you running so scared you'd rather eat a bullet than face it?"

"You want to know? Fine, I'll tell you. Then you can analyze me all you want." She threw the gun at him and he caught it to his chest. "I was out on patrol, me and one of the men they'd sent me from headquarters who knew the lay of the land. Little did I know they'd been sent there to take us out, to lead us to our deaths."

~~~

Coop watched her pace as she talked. He knew, for whatever reason, he'd pushed her too far. But he couldn't back away now. If he did he might as well shoot her himself. He slid the gun to the back of his pants, leaned against the tree, and waited.

"Shipley and I hadn't trusted them from the get-go. There was something...something off about their knowledge of the area. They knew it. Not like they lived there, but had studied a map." Her snort made him smile. "I could read a fucking map."

He watched her pace more, her face a study in concentration. The moon danced across her face each time she turned toward it and took his breath away.

"Then that last day, we heard the chopper overhead. The men, Davidson and Hurley, seemed relieved. That, of course, put us all on alert. But we had a job to do, extract the hostages."

"How many?" She looked at him, startled, as if she'd forgotten he was there until he spoke. "How many hostages were you to get out?"

"Five. We'd done it before. That was our assignment. That's all we did, actually. Go in, kill the fuck-tards willing to give up their lives for a few bucks, and get the friendlies out. But this time was different. They'd taken our personals. All of them...most of them."

"Personals? I don't...your ID's?"

She continued pacing, answering his question without thought. "Cells, clothes, packs—anything and everything that they wouldn't have to bring back when we were dead were to be left behind. We'd had to leave it at the last entry point…the last unit we'd been at. But I didn't trust them, none of us did. We each had a drop, a cell we kept paid up but not on, nothing traceable. We took them with us everywhere. The only people who knew the numbers were people we trusted." She frowned. "Or I guess people we thought we could trust. The moment we turned them on they were all over us."

He knew she'd never thought this through before. He could see by the look on her face that it had never occurred to her that whoever had the cell numbers had betrayed them. He thought she'd make a hell of a detective. Prickly one, but a good one.

"The men showed up first, then later the goon squad. I don't remember them, I'd already been hurt, already been…Shipley told me later they wanted them to leave the area, get on a chopper and hand over their weapons. They wouldn't leave me…leave without at least my body. So my men…the men disarmed them and held them until they did. Find me, that is. David showed up about that time." She looked at him. "David, I trust. He was too…those men, they were sent by someone. They said…"

"Said what, Sydney? What did they tell you?" She started pacing and instead of answering him, she continued on.

"I was making my final sweep before lights out. Davidson had come along. He said he wanted to point out something he'd seen earlier. Something that wasn't bad, just curious. I had a thought to say no, but something happened. Something he said…" She paced more. He could see she was trying to remember. "He said something about his mother."

His mother? "So he was a native. His mother was nearby?" Coop wished he had a pen and paper. He was trying to remember as many details as he could.

"No, that's not it. It's something else. The first shot hit me in the chest. I wasn't even aware it was a bullet until the second one hit me. I drew and turned on him at the same time and shot. He dropped immediately. I guess we'd been walking for about twenty clicks when this happened. The next bullet hit my head. I remember falling, thinking this is it. But I didn't black out. I couldn't hear, but I didn't black out."

Three shots, he knew there were more because she'd been shot seven times and beaten up. He waited, knowing that she wouldn't hear him even if he asked her. She was reliving the story now and in deep.

~~~

"His body hit mine, it was just there. His fists were banging away at me, my face, arms. I knew there was someone…more than one, I guess, that came up behind him. The man on me, he tumbled forward and fell off." She stopped suddenly and closed her eyes. "My gun jammed. The man standing said, 'my gun jammed. Beating you to shit wasn't supposed to happen.' Can't explain that away as unfriendly. I stared up at him, wondering who he was, what he wanted. I reached for my gun, but he kicked it away. 'Can't have that now, can we, Sydney?' the man had said. 'You and your team have to disappear. You've made too much noise to all the wrong people. But for you…killing you, I get an extra bonus….'"

"My men won't go easy. They'll find you."

His laughter rang around them as he looked down. Then he leaned down before he spoke again. "Your men are already dead, my dear. They just don't know it yet. The team that lands in twenty minutes will make sure there isn't enough left to identify once we're finished."

The gun at her waist, the one she'd kept hidden, was out and at his chest before he could think. Sin shot him twice concurrently. She let him drop on her, not knowing what was still out there and who might come up next.

The next shot fired hit in the dirt next to her head, spraying undergrowth into her face. She lay still, not sure where it had come from other than it was in front of her. She closed her eyes when she heard a twig break close to her. Pain had her coming up immediately as something snapped her leg.

Not looking, she was sure whoever it was had taken it off at the knee. Firing wildly, she knew she hit him when he yelled out in pain. Lying back down, she waited. He would either shoot in her direction or not, depending on how badly he was hurt.

Pain woke her again. She must have blacked out because she wasn't sure what had happened for several seconds when something hit her again, this time low in the belly. The muzzle flash had her firing again, but she couldn't see much. Blurring images kept shifting around her. After firing again, she knew that she would soon run out of ammo if she continued.

Dizzy now, she couldn't hold her eyes open; her body was losing blood. She pulled out her cell, but couldn't make the numbers come into focus. Blood on her fingers and her shaking hands made her drop it. She felt the world tilt back and forth then she was out again.

The next time she woke, she was being dragged. A man had her by the boot and was pulling her along behind him. She put her hand on her belly wound and found her gun. He must have thought she was dead or he'd checked and found her to be too far gone to worry with. Lifting the gun took more energy than she had, but she knew that wherever he was taking her, she wasn't going to come back from it. Lifting the gun up, she fired until the slide came back, signaling she was empty. If anyone else came, she was dead, she thought.

"They said you'd been shot seven times. Seven times, yet you managed to take out six men."

She looked at him for several seconds, her gaze slightly unfocused.

"Sydney?"

"Six men? I don't…I don't remember. They wouldn't tell me anything until I told them what had happened." She sat down on the log near her and leaned back on her hands. "I think they were there to do just what he said, take out my team. I've been trying to figure out who would pay a bonus to have me done in. I have some…people looking into some things. Nothing so far."

~~~

He moved over to her and sat down. He was close enough that he could smell her shampoo, strawberries, he thought. Shifting, he moved to face her, his legs on either side of the log and her between them. Coop had never wanted a woman so badly in his life. When she stood up he nearly whimpered, but said nothing.

"I have to go in now." Nervous, she was nervous, he could tell. "You can keep the gun." She turned to go and was about five feet away when he stopped her, but she didn't turn.

"Sydney?" He stood up. "This isn't over between us. You started something out here tonight and I mean to find out why you felt the need to take your life."

She didn't move for several seconds then without turning, she told him. "I found out yesterday that I can't have children. They said that when I'd been shot, there had been too much damage done to make my fallopian tubes viable. I told...I told it to that guy I've been seeing. He told me...he said damaged goods wasn't worth his time no matter how much my family was worth."

He sat there for a while after she'd left, not really believing that someone could be so callous as to say that to a person who had nearly given her life for her country—his country. Coop pulled out his cell and made a call.

"Do you fucking know what time it is? If you don't have your blood all over your body, then you will shortly if you don't have a fucking good reason for calling me at the butt fuck of midnight."

Allen Cramer was a charmer, no doubt about it. "No blood, not yet at any rate. You up for shedding some in the name of a pretty woman?"

He didn't answer, but he could hear him shifting in his bed. Then Coop heard him tell someone that he'd be back in a minute. A door shut then Allen was back on the line.

"Must be a very pretty girl if you're calling me and breaking silence. Who is she and what does she mean to you? And if you tell me this is just one of your fuck buddies I won't believe you. You don't even fix parking tickets for them."

He trusted Allen with his life. But did he trust him with his love life? Only one way to find out. "She's becoming very important to me. Seriously very important."

The noise at the other end had him jerking the phone from his ear. He wasn't sure what it was until Allen came back on the line. "'Bout fucking time. Anything. Tell me what you need and it's yours. Fuck yeah! Payton Cooperider has met his match. Wait until I tell Cindi. She'll have a cow, two—"

"You can't tell anyone, remember? I'm in hiding, you dork." Coop smiled when Allen started cussing. "You kiss your wife with that mouth? Christ, I miss you."

"I miss you too, cocksucker. When we get this guy Wickett, I'm going to personally piss in his face. Give me the name and what you want done."

Coop gave him everything he could on the guy, including his plate number. "I want him to suffer and loudly, understand? And you have to remain clear. It will come back to bite my ass if you don't."

After a few more minutes of conversation, Coop went into the house to find Sydney. Smiling, he realized the conversation they were having was far from over.

~Chapter 10~

Sin paced her room. It didn't take her long to get from one side to the other, but that was fine too. She just wanted to burn energy, not walk a hundred miles or so. She heard Coop come down the stairs and then her door opened.

"I'm going to bed. Will you join me?" He leaned against the door frame as he asked her. "I'd say let's use your bed, but I doubt I could lay on it alone much less with you and what I have a mind to do with you."

She could only stare at him for a minute. "Are you fucking nuts? I'm not sleeping with you. I don't even know why I didn't shoot you out there. Speaking of which, I want my gun back." She put out her hand hoping he'd just give it to her, but it was too much to hope for. But he did take her hand and bring it to his mouth. His breath was hot and his tongue curled around her fingers as he watched her face. Her body responded hard. Her nipples tightened, her pussy creamed, and she felt her pulse triple. Jerking her hand back, she stared at him.

"You can come and get it from me. I'll be more than glad to give it to you if you promise to come to bed with me. Oh, and Sydney, I don't plan on sleeping with you either. When you come to my bed, we'll be making love all night." With a quick kiss to her mouth, he left her.

She wanted to scream. She wanted to kick something, preferably him. But most of all, she wanted to follow him, to find out if he could go all night and to see if what Taylor had told her about Cooper being a Dom was true.

Sin sat on her bed. The doctor had told her that she was young and healthy and that she would have no problem adopting as many children as she wanted. But having a child, carrying one for nine months, was too dangerous for her and the child. Sin lay back on the bed.

If it were just her, she'd chance it. If she ever found a man she could marry. She knew the chances of that happening were slim to none. But it was what he'd said after that had made her so depressed that she decided to eat her own bullet.

"Miss Waite, you won't be able to work either. I've already got the paperwork for you to fill out and send in. With the damage done to your body...well, you're just lucky that you can walk and get around. The Army has agreed to pay you until your death. I would stay at home and find a hobby."

A hobby? What the fuck was she supposed to do, glue pictures in a book and put some pretty crap around it? She didn't have a problem with that sort of thing. It just wasn't her. She thought about all the girly things her sisters did. She had never even owned a doll much less a pet. She had held her nephew for three minutes the other day and all he did was scream at the top of his lungs the entire time. Quinn said it was because she was so scared and he could feel it. Well no fucking shit. He'd read that right; she was scared. Give her a fucking gun or a knife and she'd be better off.

When she felt the tears rolling down her cheeks again she looked over at the clock on the floor. It had been over an hour since Payton had left her. She figured he would be asleep by now. She got up, stripped down to her skivvies, and pulled on her blacks. She would simply sneak into his room and get her weapon. She knew she wouldn't be able to sleep without it in here anyway. Ten minutes later she was creeping up the stairs.

She realized when she opened the first door and it wasn't his that she really didn't have any clue where he might have been sleeping since he'd moved in. She was on the third one when she found him.

She knew that he'd been in her room. She hadn't served in the Army for so long that she hadn't learned to protect what was hers. Nothing had been touched, nothing moved, but the door was different. He'd closed it when he'd left.

She moved across the room in the shadows. He was breathing slowly and she knew to listen to the slightest change. She was nearly to his bed when he rolled to his back. She froze where she was until he started to snore slightly. She wanted to brain him for rolling over. It was harder to look in his bed with him spread out like he owned the place. She moved closer and went down on her knee. She was just reaching under his mattress where she knew he'd hid it when she was suddenly flying through the air and on his bed with him on top of her.

"Hi. Changed your mind I see," he said with humor. When he started to roll away she tried to escape, but he was back before she could move. He brought her hands to the top of the bed and she heard a rasping noise. Then there was a cuff around her wrist.

When she jerked on the cuff she realized he'd just handcuffed her to the bed. "Let me the fuck go. Right now, or so help me, I'll make you regret it."

"Not yet. And when I'm finished with you, if you still want to leave, then I will gladly let you go. But I've wanted you for entirely too long to let you out of my bed just yet."

His mouth was everywhere. Her neck, her arms; even through her clothes she felt his bites, his nips at her. She wanted to protest, to beg him to stop, but she wasn't sure she'd get anything more than begging and it wouldn't be to stop.

His hands at her pants had her shifting away, but he didn't stop. When she felt the slide of the zipper go down she knew that he was going to have her. She was glad for the dark. Since she couldn't see him, she knew he couldn't see her.

"Not speaking, baby?" His voice was a whisper against her belly. "Okay, I'll just tell you what I'm going to do. First, I'm going to take off your clothes. I know it will be difficult with you cuffed this way. That's why I left your one hand lose. But I promise it won't interfere with what I'm going to do to you."

Her pants opened and she felt his mouth on her hip. When he pulled them down her legs he took her briefs with them. Socks came off as well. She heard them hit the floor to her right.

"Please don't do this, Mr. Cooper. It's not—"

He flipped her from her back and swatted her bare ass. The pain was incredible. And before she could tell him so, he hit her again and again. She was sure now that he'd been pegged correctly, but if he thought she was going to go submissively into his coils he was sadly mistaken. She tried to flip back over, but he straddled her legs and held her there with his weight. When his hands started to massage her abused cheeks she couldn't help the moan that spilled from her mouth.

"Are you wet, Sydney? Did my spanking you make you wet for me? Let me see." She felt his fingers slide down her ass cheeks and between her thighs. She tried to tighten her legs together, but he was inside of her before she could manage to make her body cooperate with her will.

His fingers filled her. And before she knew it she was arching her ass up to meet each of his strokes. When his breath was on her ass she moaned again.

"Hummm, you smell delicious. I want to taste you, baby. Will you let me? Will you let me fuck your wet pussy with my tongue and drink from you?" She couldn't answer. Her body was on fire so she lifted her ass up higher and offered it to him. "Answer me, baby. You have to say yes. But before you do, you should know that I'm not going to just want to hear 'yes' from you. I want all of you. You're mine, Sydney. No more Mr. Cooper, no more telling me to stop. You're mine. Do you understand what I'm telling you?"

"Yes, you think I'm going to be your slave. Well, I may be horny, but not horny enough to beg any man to be my master." He didn't move from her body for several seconds and she thought she'd won, but then he was gone from her.

"Too bad. I need you to be my sub." He pulled her shirt up and over her head. "But I'm not giving up on you. You beg me right and I'll give you the most pleasure you've ever had."

"You're awfully sure of yourself, aren't you? I want you to let me go." She heard the rustle of clothes and thought he was going to leave her. "You can't do this to me. Let me go right this minute."

When he lay down beside her and pulled her close she fought him. When he simply threw his leg over her hips, she couldn't move. He was naked. Reaching out with her free hand she tried to scratch at him, but he grabbed her wrist and held it over her head.

"Behave or I'll cuff your other wrist. I mean it. No play time unless they're by my rules or we sleep. Which is it going to be?"

"I fucking hate you," she said through her teeth. "You're *so* going to pay for this."

His laughter made her madder. "You shouldn't threaten a man who has you naked and tied to his bed, love. You might just get spanked again. Are you going to behave, Sydney, or do I get the other handcuff out?"

She jerked her hand from him and laid it on her chest. His chuckle made her grind her teeth, but she didn't speak.

He kissed her nipple and then laved it with his tongue. When he snuggled between her breasts she could feel his cock against her thigh and nearly begged him to take her any way he wanted. He was thick and hot against her and she wanted, wanted so badly, to have him deep inside of her.

"Good night, love."

~~~

Coop waited for her to fall asleep before he moved away. His cock hurt, ached so badly that he was tempted to go to the bathroom and jerk off. He looked down at her body and the way the moonlight from the window bathed her in it. She was simply the most beautiful creature he'd ever seen. Groaning, he got up.

He stood next to the bed and looked down at her with his cock in his hand. To come all over her this way was something he'd thought about a great deal; her taking him down her throat was another way. In her ass, her pussy; hell, he wanted to fuck those beautiful breasts and watch his cum shoot all over her face when he came. Taking a deep breath, he stepped back. This was *so* not helping. He went into the bathroom and stood in front of the mirror. Now what?

He'd hoped she'd come for the gun. He didn't know what he have done if she'd really wanted loose, but when she arched into his hand when he'd spanked her he knew he'd done the right thing. She was his. He wasn't ready to admit that she had been his from the moment he'd seen her, but she had. He turned on the shower behind him to cold and didn't even wait to see if he was going to die from the chill, but stepped under the freezing spray.

By the time his feet were numb and his fingers too, he figured he'd be able to go back to bed with her. Wrapping the towel around his waist, he walked back to the bed. He tried not to look at her, but couldn't help it. She was just lying there sleeping in his bed, handcuffed, and he wanted her all over again. Trying not to snuggle into her warmth so he wouldn't wake her, he was pleased when she kept coming back to him. By the time he was getting warm again she was nearly on top of him and he was hard again. He never thought he'd get to sleep, but within minutes he drifted off.

When he opened his eyes she was staring at him. It was morning he could tell, but how late he wasn't sure. He wanted to pull her back into his arms like she'd been last night, but there was a look in her eye that frankly scared him.

"Morning. How'd you sleep? I slept like the dead." He rolled over and on top of her to see if she would speak to him. "Do you like morning sex, or are you strictly a night sex person? I can do it with you all day and not be tired."

"I have to pee. Can you please get the fuck off me and let me go? I've had enough of your shit for three lifetimes." She wiggled around to try and throw him off, but all she managed to do was make him harder. "Do you mind?"

"Nope. I'll let you up to go to the bathroom. And you can shower, but you aren't leaving me. We have some things to work out between us and one of them is how you're going to be up here from now on and not in that little room." He moved off her and to the side of the bed. Her moan had him look back at her. She was staring at his cock. "You've no idea what you do to me seeing you there like that. I wanted to jerk off on you last night, come all over your luscious body. Christ, baby, I want you so badly."

He moved back to the side of the bed and ran his finger down her ribs then up again. Her nipples hardened under his stare and he moved back down to take the tiny morsel into his mouth. Her breasts tightened and she moved her legs closed.

"You want me, Sydney? You want me to make you come?" Still nothing. He could wait her out...he hoped. Pulling back he let her nipple pop out of his mouth and he moved to stand again. "You have to beg me, love. Let's get you in the shower, shall we?"

He had a moment when he nearly let her go. While he'd been leaning over her to unlock the cuff she'd used her free hand to wrap around his cock. He watched her hand as it rode up and down him until he could feel the impending climax begin to tingle up his balls. He pulled back and finished uncuffing her. He locked the cuff he'd just taken off the bed on his own wrist and smiled at her expression.

"You didn't think I'd just let you go, did you? Shame on you. I'm not near as far gone as that. Though I will tell you, having you touch me that way has made me decide to give you a reward." He helped her stand then rubbed her arm until he could tell it no longer hurt. "First bathroom, then shower. You wash my back, I'll wash yours."

"I'm not taking a shower with you. You have to let me go...I can't, you can't mean to bathe with me." Panic was something he didn't think to see on her face or hear in her voice. "This is stupid, Mr…Payton, let me go now."

He didn't answer, but took her to the bathroom and turned on the water. "I'll have my back to you while you use the toilet then you can step in the stall while I use it. But please don't flush or we'll be taking a cold shower."

He knew the moment she decided that he wasn't giving up. He felt her tug on his arm twice, but he was sure it was from normal use and not trying to get away. When he felt her stand he moved so she could enter the stall then he stood and used the commode as well. Closing the lid, he hoped that he'd be able to do this or he was going to take her hard against the wall. Moving the curtain back, he got in behind her.

Her back was to him and he stepped up behind her and wrapped his arm around her waist. He could tell she was crying, but he couldn't let her go. He needed her, and in some twisted way he thought she needed him as well.

Reaching up over her head he pulled the shampoo down and poured some into his hand. He felt he also needed to clear the air between them, no more lies. It was trust her or not.

"I have to tell you something. Something that could get me killed. I know I'm taking a big chance telling you at this moment because I'm sure you'd just as soon do the job yourself as to turn me over to the bad guys, but I don't want any lies between us when we make love."

"We aren't going to make love. You hate me as much as I hate you. And I don't want your life history. As soon as this is over I'm having you arrested." He nipped at her shoulder as he began to wash her hair. "And I don't want you to dominate me. I don't want sex with you either."

"You said that," he said with a smile. "But you have to hear my story. I'm a cop. A detective, actually. I was shot on the job about two months ago. I was on a buy; drugs were being distributed at the local middle school and I was set up by my boss to purchase then arrest this low end guy hoping he'd talk. My captain set it up, the buy, the meeting place, everything."

"Let me guess, he wasn't a trustworthy sort of guy. Been there, done that. Someone sent me and my guys out without any backup and I got hurt too. No one is to be trusted anymore." She rattled the cuffs between them. "Not even some guy who steals your gun."

He swatted her ass. "Behave and listen. And you were ready to come last night when I had you tied to the bed. Where was I…oh yeah. He told me not to take my phone too. So being the by the book bastard I am, I took my cell phone. The buyer didn't show. But someone did. I was shot and while I'm lying there ready to die Wickett comes over the radio and tells me that he's in the back pocket of—"

"Did you say Wickett? Carl Wickett?" She had turned so quickly that his arm was now wrapped around her waist and hers was behind her. But it was her quiet question that startled him.

"Yes. He's my captain. You…how did you know?" Her eyes closed as she leaned against the stall wall. "Sydney? What is it?"

103

"He was married to Quinn if it's the same guy." She looked up at him. "Sort of average height, blond hair, green eyes, maybe has a scar just over his left eye."

Coop nodded. He couldn't say much just yet. Quinn, he'd met her at the hospital. She was married to the attorney. "Was he a cop here?"

"Yes. He beat her. Quinn, he beat her all the time. I was on leave when he...I trained her how to defend herself with him. We went to the gym three, four times a week when he was in the hospital on another injury. Might have been job related or not, who knew with him. I had to go back before her...she nearly killed him. He was in intensive care for nearly a month, Cain told me. When Wacky Wickett was out, he disappeared. Never heard from him again. He went to wherever you're from."

"Jersey. He was an officer when I was in school then got a promotion just after I joined the force. Wacky Wickett? Suits him." He looked down at her and wanted to kiss her. "I'm hiding here until I heal. He's looking for me because I can testify against him about this shooting and another."

"He's not too stupid, but you have to know he'll come here sometime if he figures it out. What's your connection to here? Cain or something or someone else?"

Coop wanted to be impressed with her figuring it out, but all he could think about was that he might have led the bastard right to her. "My mom is a cousin to...holy Christ. Thomas Miller. Miller, isn't that Quinn's husband's name?"

She nodded then started to giggle. Then that turned into a full laugh. At first, he couldn't figure out what the hell was so funny then it hit him. "We're all connected. All of us, we're all connected."

She looked up at him with laughter still on her face and Coop fell in love. He figured he'd been falling all along, but it hit him hard in the belly and his heart. Leaning down, he kissed her. Kissed her like she belonged to him and him to her. When he pulled away but not back, he leaned his forehead on hers before he spoke.

"My name is Payton Riley Cooperider. My mother...my mom is Candace Cooperider, always Candace, never Candy, and my dad, Payton the second, died about ten years ago in the line of duty. My sister, Shaller Hall, divorced, lived in New York until I got hurt and now she lives with mom. I call them both once a week on a pay as you go phone or she'll kick my ass. I'm so sorry, baby. I never meant to—"

Her mouth covered his.

~Chapter 11~

Sin wanted him. Not because he was there, but because he'd shared with her. She wasn't even sure that was it either, but she did want him. Shifting around, she moved him back against the stall and took his mouth again. When he cupped her ass and brought her hard against his erection she threw back her head and moaned.

"Christ, I need to taste you. Now." Coop dropped her feet back to the floor and helped her steady. When he started to drop to the floor too, she stopped him.

"Are you...are you really a Dom like Taylor said you were?" At his confused look, she went on. "The other day when we met for dinner she said her and Byron had you pegged as a Dom and me your sub. They own some clubs. Tightly Banded, I think."

"Tightly Bound. Yes. I know the club and yes, I'm a Dom. I have been in some form or another most of my life." He brushed her hair out of her face as he continued. "I won't hurt you, Sydney...well, I will, but I won't harm you. I want you to enjoy this time between us too. The thought of tying you down and taking you hard and fast makes me want to do it now. But if you don't…if you can't then I won't. Not with you."

She wasn't afraid of him; it was herself she was afraid of. The thought of him tying her down didn't bother her; it was her liking it too much that scared her. She told him this. "I don't know if I can…I've never even thought of sex like that before. Never occurred to me to seek someone out that could—"

"And you won't either. Not now." His voice was so firm she nearly laughed, but didn't. "You're mine, Sydney. I'm going to show you how to enjoy this." Coop reached over the ledge, pulled down the key to the cuffs, and handed it to her. "If you don't want this then you unlock these from us. It doesn't mean that I don't want you. It just means that we won't be playing. Understand this, though, if you put the key back you're mine in the bedroom. Always. I will defer to you outside of there; you're much more capable of what you do than me, but in here, in this room, I'm in charge."

She held the key tight in her hand. What he was offering her was more than she'd ever had from a man that wasn't in her command. Trust and a choice.

"And if I don't like it, then what do we do? I can't relock it after we start, can I?" She looked up into his face. There was so much hope there, and something else. "Payton? What if I don't enjoy this?"

"Drop to your knees and take me into your mouth. Don't lick me, don't do anything, but take me deep into your mouth and let me fuck you."

She didn't know why, but she did as he asked. As soon as her mouth wrapped around him she reached down to touch her pussy. "*No.* No, don't touch yourself and don't come. I'm going to come down your throat and if you're good, and I don't come right away, I'll reward you by eating your pussy until you come."

He rocked hard into her mouth. It was nearly too much. He was so thick and when he touched the back of her throat she nearly gagged, but swallowed hard and the reflex went away. He fucked her easy and slowly at first, but the more he did it the harder and faster he went. She wanted to taste him, swirl her tongue around his fat head and taste him, but he'd said no and she didn't want to disappoint him.

The faster he went the harder it was not to taste, not to touch. Not just herself, but him too. The thought of wrapping her hand around him and pumping him hard was nearly overwhelming. She wanted to come and the harder she tried not to think about it, the harder it became not to think. Digging her nails into her thighs helped some, but she wasn't going to make it. Just when she was ready to say screw it and bring herself to orgasm, he came.

"Yes. Baby, yes. Take my…Christ, my balls, please?"

She cupped him in her hand as he shot his hot cum down her throat. She still didn't touch him with her tongue, but his taste was there on the back of her tongue to savor. When he yanked her up by her hair and she was up, he sat down on the shower seat and turned her around so that her back was to his chest. Bending her over, he pulled her to him and buried his face between her legs.

She spread her legs when his hands pulled them apart. His finger sliding into her pussy nearly had her screaming out his name. She was close, so close that she was dizzy from it.

"Come, Sydney, come now."

Her body responded to his command. She did scream now, her voice raw with it. When he turned her around and pulled her onto his hard cock she came again and again.

Riding him now, sliding up and down on him while he sat there, she screamed again when he took her nipple into his mouth and bit her. Not hard, but enough for her to know he'd done it on purpose. When he shouted out his own release she came too, the feeling of his cum shooting deep within her too much that the room dimmed and she went limp against him.

She felt the water go off and the towel on her shoulders. Then she was being carried gently to somewhere soft and warm. She felt bad for a second. She knew that his wounds will still too new, too fresh to be carrying her weight, but it didn't matter as soon as he laid her on his bed.

"Baby, you need to wake up for me. Sydney? Wake up, please?" She wanted to sleep, not wake up. "But you need to just long enough to listen to me."

She opened one eye and stared up at him. She loved him. Smiling again, she tried to close her eye, but he shook her. "What is it? I'm tired, you wore me out." His laughter made her look at him. He held up the key. "You never answered me. What if I don't...why are you laughing?"

"Oh, honey, you liked it. You liked it very much. We'll go slow...well, as slow as I can, but you're a sub, at least here in the bedroom. But if you change your mind then we'll try to go back, but I don't think you will."

She didn't understand, but she unlocked the cuffs. Anything, she thought, to get him to let her go to sleep. As soon as she undid his wrist first he kissed her nose, then the one around her own wrist was off. She handed him the cuffs and the tiny little key. Snuggling up to him, she felt safe, warm and, for some stupid reason, pampered.

"You still need to give me back my gun. I need to have it under my pillow when I sleep." She laid her head on his chest as she spoke. "And I'm going running in the morning—ouch! That fucking hurt."

She rubbed her ass where he'd smacked her and glared. It hadn't really hurt, but it did sting a bit. She wondered if she was weird when she tried to think of something else to piss him off. Then decided she didn't care and opened her mouth to blast him.

"Think hard on that. We're still in the bedroom. And I won't stop with a slap to that fine ass of yours. I will make you suffer in ways you can't even imagine." She closed her mouth. "Good girl. Now, your gun is under your pillow as mine is under mine. I understand that need. But you will not try again what you did tonight, Sydney. I won't have it, understand me?"

Tears filled her eyes. "You've no idea what he said to me. You've…he called me worthless as a human. He told me I was worthless."

"I took care of his ass. You sleep now. I've got your back. Always."

Sin had never been one to cry herself to sleep, but tonight she did. And it didn't feel shameful because someone had witnessed it either. Payton held her close to him and stroked her back until she fell asleep. She didn't think she'd sleep a wink.

Something was wrong. She didn't move, couldn't think where she was, what had happened. A moan to her left had her moving her head that way slowly. She could make out a figure on a chair, but nothing more. When he moaned again, she let out a long breath. It was Payton.

"I'm sorry. I didn't mean to wake you. Go back to sleep." She got up. He could spank her if he wanted, but she didn't care. "My leg, I guess I did too much today. It hurts like a mother fucker."

She sat at his feet and started to massage his foot. Hard strokes up and down the top and bottom. "Do you have anything for pain?"

"Yeah, but I'll get it in a minute. That feels good." She smacked his thigh then reached over and turned the lamp on. "What the hell?"

"Don't be stupid. Where are they and what do you need to take them with?" She stood up to go and get them. "I mean it, this has nothing to do with sex. This is pain and pain management. You need something and I'm going to make sure you get it."

He laid back and closed his eyes and she knew he should have had something some time ago. "Downstairs in the glass cabinet. I just drink some of your tea. And before you take my head off, I did a great deal of things tonight that I haven't done in a while, including carrying you to bed."

She leaned down and kissed his mouth quickly. "I wasn't. But it's nice to know you think I can. I'll be back."

She was nearly to the door when she realized she was naked. She turned back to get something to pull on and saw his shirt. "Do you care if I pull this on until I get back?"

"No. Can I ask what you normally sleep in?" He watched her walk across the floor and she bent at the waist to lean over and pick up his shirt her ass to him. His groan made her smile.

"Shipley, a guy who was under me in command, gave me some of his fatigues to wear. I think I have several of them. I sleep in one of them and a pair of issued briefs. Why?"

"You'll not be wearing them to my bed. Especially another man's clothes. In fact, I would be happy if you wore nothing at all. Come here." She shook her head. "Sydney, don't refuse me."

"I'm going to get your pain pills. I know you want me. Christ, I want you too. But we both know the pain will only get worse. After the drugs, if you still want me I'll sit on your cock right there in the chair and make you scream with release."

She left the room before she could see what he thought of that. She was still very nervous about this domination thing and whether or not she'd—

She was nearly to the bottom of the stairs when she stopped.

He'd already done it. In the shower he'd made her do what he wanted and she'd done it. Smiling to herself she went on to the kitchen. Okay, so she liked it. Reading the bottle of medicine that had his name on it, she poured a glass of tea for him and took a sip of it. Setting it down, she pulled off his shirt and put it in the laundry area. Naked again, she took the bottle and the glass back up to his room.

His eyes were closed when she entered. She knew he wasn't asleep; he was still massaging his leg. When he looked up at her she could see the hunger in his eyes. She handed him the bottle and the glass and watched him look at her.

"If you take only what you need I'd really like to help you get your mind off the pain for a little while. I was thinking I'd very much like you to let me suck on your cock this time."

He watched her sit at his feet again and looked at her for a minute before he spoke softly. "You figured out you like being my sub."

"Yes. Very clever of you, that. How did you know?" She started rubbing her hands up and down his thighs and watched his cock dance on his groin. "I mean, did I say something or do something that told you?"

"Not really. I guess it was hope more than…Sydney, are you going to suck on my cock or not?"

She grinned at him. "You didn't take your pill, nor did you say I could. Do you want me to call you master?"

"Yes."

She wrapped her hand around his cock and licked the tip. She thought his eyes rolled all the way around his head before he looked at her again. "Yes that I can, or yes I should call you master? You have to be very clear on these things. I wouldn't want to get beaten again." She licked him from balls to tip, swirling her tongue around him before she pulled back. "Payton?"

"Yes to both. Take me now before I come all over your face." She rose up, but before she could move over him, he stopped her. "You're going to be punished as soon as I'm not in so much pain. And if you don't know why, then you'll get it twice as badly."

She put her knees on either side of his thighs and held his cock in her hand as she rubbed him back and forth in her juices. Before she sat down on him she looked him in the eye. "Yes, master."

~~~

Coop was sure his heart stopped beating and his breathing quit. She was tight and hot and when she moved forward on him again he grabbed her hips to slow her down. Leaning forward slightly, he took her nipple in his mouth and suckled just on the hard tip. When her hands gripped his shoulders he nearly stood up to take her against the wall where he could pound into her.

"No. Your leg won't…fuck, you feel good in me." He pulled her tighter to him and reached around to her ass. "Yes, please. Please, Payton."

He smacked her hard. "Master. Say it. Call me master." He hit her again and again.

"Please, master. I need…fuck me, please."

Coop reached behind her and slid his fingers into the seam of her ass. He couldn't wait to fuck her here, his cock in her tight hole. Bringing his free hand to her pussy, he pinched her clit twice before gathering her cream and then rubbing it into her ass.

"I'm going to fuck you here soon. We'll need to make a trip to Bound and get some toys for us." His thumb broke through the tight muscle. "Has anyone taken you here before, slave? Anyone fucked this tight ass of yours?"

"No. Please. Please, I need to come. Let me come." She was riding him hard, but he needed more from her. He wanted to come on her, not in her this time.

"Slave, I want you to get on your knees in front of me. I'm going to fuck your mouth and come all over you. I want to watch my cum drip off you." She didn't move for a second. "Slave?"

She moved off him without a word and sat the way he told her. When she closed her eyes and opened her mouth he knew he couldn't last. Scooting forward to the edge of the chair he grabbed his cock and fisted himself hard.

"Fuck, I'm coming." The first stream hit her in the mouth and she licked it. His cock surged and he came painfully hard. Her breasts, her chin, even her eyes were being covered. When a long stream of it dripped from her nipple Coop felt his body come again, his balls giving up all of him in a final spurt that hit her in the mouth again. As he watched her, she rubbed his cum into her breasts and chin; she lapped her fingers until they were clean of him. Not about to let that go, he grabbed her to him and kissed her, tasting him on her tongue.

"Please. Help me. Please? I hurt, master."

She needed to come and he knew it. He thought about letting her suffer for teasing him, but found he wanted to taste her cum too. Standing her up he pulled her pussy to his mouth and fucked her clit with his tongue. She came with a scream. When he pushed his finger deep into her pussy he used his other hand to do the same to her ass. She grabbed his head and held on as he fucked her hard this way. When she came again and again he knew he'd found his mate, his other half, his sub.

When she finally pulled away he let her go. He was a bit wobbly himself. Standing up, he helped her to the bed, both of them leaning heavily on each other until they were settled. He didn't remember to take his pain pill and he doubted he'd ever need one again if she was willing to be his distraction. Smiling, Coop fell into a deep sleep.

~Chapter 12~

Roger moved among the other people in the airport and found a seat near the food court. He'd been here before, twice now since he'd landed in Ohio three days ago, and he had the information needed. When he saw his contact coming toward him, he gave a small shake of his head and picked up his coffee. Not yet.

David stayed back and waited. When Roger saw the other man coming toward him he nodded, set his coffee down, and picked up the envelope he'd had ready. This man was who he was waiting on.

"You find him yet? The boss said to tell you he would like for you to hurry your ass along." The man flopped down in the chair across from Roger. "Where'd you get that crap at?"

"It's coffee. And yes. Tell him I have an address for where he was last time he was here. There's a hospital on Central that caters to the druggies here and he was sent there by his chief and someone else, I think his mother. I'm still trying to find Wickett's missing wife, but by all accounts she disappeared a few months ago. Left the country. Still trying to find more on her."

Roger didn't tell him she was married or that she'd left to go on her honeymoon then later to visit his captain. Roger left that bit of news out of his report too. At least to this party. It was beginning to look like Wickett was in deeper and deadlier than they had first thought. Everyone was. When the man left, Roger got up and headed to the head…the bathroom.

Getting used to civilian life was proving to be much harder than he'd first thought it would be. The people were all right, he supposed, if not a bit over taxed. They all seemed to use their cell phones as if they were their lifelines. A lot more people carried guns, and a great deal of them were women. And coffee, the one thing he missed on assignment more than anything, was getting harder and harder to find. Oh, he supposed he could get any kind of fat free with a hundred different names attached to it, but good old coffee? Not happening.

He was urinating when David moved in to one of the stalls behind him. When he came out he washed his hands, laid an envelope on the counter, and took the one there with him. After he was finished Roger slipped the envelope under his shirt then washed up. His first contact came in just as he was shaking the water off his fingers.

"Forget something?" The guy started looking under the stall door and then when he was apparently satisfied he drew a gun. "You thinking of using that, pencil dick?"

"I don't like you much. The boss told me that if I wasn't met by you today then I was to hunt you down and make you understand he pays the bills. I don't think you've been here once over the past couple of days." He waved his gun to the right and Roger didn't move. "I want you over in that stall."

"Nope." Roger threw his paper towel in the trash as he continued. "You been lying to the boss, huh? Not too terribly smart of you. Especially since he called me last night and asked me if you were showing up."

"You lie! He said you didn't have his number. Said you were a piece of shit and he wanted you dead." The man's eyes darted around the room. "I'm going to kill you and take this job over and he'll make me his number one."

"Better come up with a better story than the one you just spun out or he's gonna know why you…well, you're gonna have to kill me before you get to talk to him and I'm reasonably sure that just ain't gonna happen." Roger reached out and snatched the gun from the man. "You see, dumb fuck, my captain used to tell me, don't talk to your victim, just fucking kill 'em and move on. Could be there are two more just waiting to take his place." He snapped the man's neck. "Sounds like good advice."

Roger stuck the gun in the back of his pants and then picked up the dead man. There was no way he could leave him out like this in a busy airport so he put him in one of the stalls and pulled his trousers down around his ankles before setting out. He pulled off a wad of toilet paper and stuck it into the door seam to make the door secure. He was just going to the sink to wash up when someone else walked in. It was David.

"He followed me in here. Didn't check for ID, don't care really. Here." Roger handed him the small Glock. "I don't want this tiny pop gun. You take it."

"I'll wait a few hours and if nobody finds him, then I'll call it in. He hurt you?" Roger quirked a brow at David's question. "Okay then. See you in three days. Be careful. I'm going to follow up with Waite sometime tomorrow."

Roger wanted to ask how she was, what she was doing, but he didn't. The girl had been through enough and with this shit going down with her new squeeze, there was going to be plenty more. He didn't doubt she'd protect herself, but her family wasn't about to let her get hurt again.

"I'll get what I can. Gotta call this in. Patterson?" When David turned back before leaving the men's room Roger continued. "I know who the leak was that got her hurt. You ain't getting it until I take care of him."

David looked like he might have said something, but simply nodded and left. It wouldn't have mattered to Roger if he had an opinion or not. The man was walking around as a corpse and Roger was going to make him lie down from now on.

Just after leaving the hospital after seeing Capt the last time David had met him right outside. He'd only handed him a slip of paper then walked away, but Roger knew he was being asked to keep things on the low side. He went to the men's room and opened the paper.

"The United States Army and the President would like for you to do some special uncover work for them. I and one other will be your only contact. The pay is a grade higher than you were making, the benefits suck just as badly, and you'll be expected not to kill too many people.

The good news is you'll wear whatever you want, which you mostly did anyway, carry any weapons you want, again pretty much your standard, and you will help find the person responsible for trying to bring down your squad.

Meet me at the library on Tenth, it's that large structure with the books lined against the wall and on shelves. Be there at eight tonight if you're interested. If you aren't then I'm sorry to say, you'll be a dead man before morning.

David Patterson"

Roger had debated right up until seven-fifty that night on whether or not he wanted to chance it. He'd been followed all day, he knew it, and he knew they knew he knew...something like that. He'd been able to lose one of them, but not all. Walking up the steps to the structure he did notice that two of the cars peeled away, but another simply parked next to his car...

David stood up as Roger approached him. As David reached out his hand Roger grabbed it and pulled his body to his and turned him to face the room. Rogers's chest to his back and his arm around his neck, the other hand held a Glock to his temple.

"Call them off." David didn't say anything so Roger let up a little on his throat. "The three by the stacks, the librarian, and the little thing putting the books away next to the movies. Tell them to back off or I fucking break your neck and then have a killing spree in this library."

David seemed to relax a bit and lifted his hand slowly. All the plants, the people Roger had pegged, had moved toward the door with the exception of the girl with the cart. With a hard shake to David, Roger didn't let him go as she walked toward them.

"I'm with him." She pointed at David. "I'm going to get you what you need to complete your assignment. I don't know who you are, nor do I give a rat's ass. This man you are currently choking to death is my boss. I do what he tells me."

When she sat down and pulled out a large phone-looking thing then looked up at them both expectantly Roger simply laughed, things were not always what they seemed. He let David go, sat down in one of the reading chairs, and regarded them both.

"Not a terribly trusting sort, are you, Shipley?" David said as he sat down and rubbed his neck. "I told them you'd spot the others, but no one would listen to me."

"What the fuck do you want, Patterson? You thinking of having me re-up or some kind of shit like that? I'm out, just like you're making the best fucking leader you got." Roger reached for his smokes, almost forgetting he was quitting. "I don't owe any of you anything."

"No, you certainly don't. But someone tried to kill all of you. And someone nearly killed our friend." David nodded to the woman who handed him a file. "The man there has some connections to Captain Waite. He's her ex-brother-in-law. Carl Wickett is also the police captain in a small precinct in Jersey. He has ties, though we don't know how deep, to the mob. We know he was involved in what went down in that jungle, but not how much."

Roger threw the file on the table between them without reading it. "Sounds to me like you don't know a whole fucking lot. Send me to kill him then the problem is solved.

What the fuck you need all this cloak and dagger shit for anyway?"

The woman picked up the file and opened it. "This man here is called Hondo. He's from New Mexico. Three months ago he was put into a position to kill you. When he didn't succeed they sent in someone else, someone who was on your team."

Roger took the picture and nearly handed it back when he looked closer. "He was in our unit. He didn't last long...sniper took him out about two—fuck! You had him killed. He was killed by a friendly. We couldn't figure out how, but we knew that's what had killed him."

"Yes," David said, picking up the story. "I wasn't made aware of this until recently. After Captain Waite...Sydney was hurt I started digging. I found this and some other information as well. But since the attempted murder there's been nothing. I figured you'd be willing to help me find more answers."

Roger sat back in the chair and looked around. There was another plant there. He wondered if David was aware of it and decided to see. "The man by the desk? He one of yours?"

The woman stood up and straightened her skirt then 'accidentally' knocked over a stack of magazines. When she stood up after picking them up she was facing the desk and the man. When she put the magazines on the desk she tumbled onto Roger's lap and looked at him first. Her smile was huge.

"No, he's not. If you gentlemen will excuse me, I have something in the ladies room to take care of." When she started to stand so did Roger. He leaned down to her

throat and nipped gently. "Sir, I assure you I'm quite capable of taking care of myself."

"He's not alone. There's a man on the second floor that has a gun on you and another woman that just slipped into the ladies room. They're listening to us." Roger glanced at David. "You armed?"

"Yes. I'm not going to ask if you are. So is Sally there. And she's right, she is good." Roger nodded and put his arm around her waist as David continued. "I'll take the man on the landing."

Roger nodded again and started to the ladies room with Sally. "We're going in there together. If you can, take out the woman. If I'm right the man at the desk will follow us. Is there anyone else you see here that shouldn't be?"

She shook her head then laid it on his shoulder. "I'm not going to ask you why we're supposed to be going in the ladies room together. But I appreciate the backup."

Roger grinned and walked in the door with her. The woman who'd walked in before them was washing her hands. When she turned she had a gun on them and Sally shot her in the forehead. Seconds passed when the man at the desk walked in, his gun out. Roger slammed the door against him and he dropped his weapon. Sally handed him her gun with the silencer and he shot the man in the forehead. As they were leaving the library they heard screaming.

Roger wrapped his arm around Sally's neck and pulled her close enough to whisper. He didn't want to take the chance she would get hurt. He didn't know this woman and he wasn't sure of her ability to fight in hand-to-hand combat. Captain would have kicked his ass if he had tried this stunt.

"David will have to get himself out of this mess. You and I are going to get out while the getting is good." They were nearly to the door when several people started running toward them, one of them David. "Don't look at him as he passes us."

Sally led him to a car and opened the door. She reached inside and opened her trunk. Walking to the back of it, she pulled Roger into her arms and with her lips nearly touching his he felt her slip something into his jacket pocket. "That's a secure phone. The only numbers programmed in it are mine and David's. Call one of us in twenty-four and tell us what your decision is. Things are getting—"

He kissed her. Roger felt justified in the action. She was lovely, close, and her mouth was right there. When she opened under the exploration of his lips, he leaned her against her car and took full advantage. He felt the bite of a gun in his belly.

When he pulled back but didn't let go he grinned down at her. "Can't blame a man for trying, sweetheart."

She huffed at him. "And you can't blame me for wanting this to be strictly professional. Twenty-four hours, Mr. Shipley."

He pulled her back for another kiss before answering. "I don't need it. I'll do it. And it's Roger or Shipley, never 'Mr.'"

That had been nine months ago. He'd been told he needed to get closer to Wickett and to make himself invaluable to him. The people he now worked for gave him all the new identity crap he needed. Now instead of Honorably Discharged as he'd been he had a "dis" added to his honorable part. And he'd been put out to pasture because he had been a rogue.

~~~

David sat in the office of the accountant. He didn't need the stupid prick, but he did need to be able to see when Sydney went into the office directly across from this office. She had an appointment at ten, which was in three minutes. He was afraid she wasn't going to show. David was just covering his watch back up with his sleeve when she stepped off the elevator. She wasn't alone. David smiled.

He had had the young man, "Coop," as he'd been called, thoroughly checked out. He knew why he was here, when he had arrived, and who was looking for him. He'd also been happy to hear from one of the men he had watching her house that the two of them seemed to be getting along rather well. He stood up just as his name was called.

Ignoring the woman, he stepped into the hall and was thrown against the wall hard. He looked up at the gun Sydney had at his forehead before he spoke.

"So I see that civilian life hasn't cooled your temperament for acting first and kicking ass later. Want to take the gun from my head before I get hurt?" The man behind her laughed, but didn't move. "Hello, Coop. Nice seeing you here."

"Fuck you, David. You knew I'd bring him. What the fuck do you think you're doing setting up bogus doctor's appointments in this building?" David looked at her.

"Yeah, I knew it was either you or some other dumb fuck that wants a piece of me. Speak up before my finger gets a cramp."

"Do you think we can do this in a less public place?" David nodded as best he could to the door across from them. "That room has been debugged and no cameras."

She looked up at the camera above them. "That one's not working either. Why do you think I'm late? You really think I'm that stupid?"

She pulled the gun away from his head, but didn't put it away. David moved from the wall and that's when he noticed that Coop had his gun out as well, only his was a little more discreet. David shook his head as the three of them entered the office. Sally was there sitting in one of the chairs and David could see she'd been busy. There were pictures hanging all around the room.

"Hello. I'm Sally. I'm going to be giving you both information on what's going on and I will be your contact from now—"

"Whoa there, kid. I don't give two shits what you think you might be, but right now I want answers from him." Sydney pointed her gun at David. "If he blows wind up my ass then whatever you say just don't mean squat to me."

"Well, you're just a rude bitch, aren't you?"

David started to tell Sally to back off, but Coop grabbed his arm.

"Yeah, that's me in a nutshell. And I would imagine you can be too if necessary. Sit." Sally had started to stand, but immediately sat back down when Sydney pointed the gun in her direction. "I was lured here for a bogus appointment; the building has more people watching it than an episode of the *Playboy* channel, David comes out of an office I know is a crook, and you want me to listen to whatever it is you have to say as if I'm supposed to need it."

David laughed. "You always were too smart for your own good. You're being followed and someone wants you dead."

~Chapter 13 ~

Sin knew she was being followed. Whoever it was had been doing it now for a few days. She'd noticed him the day after her and Payton had started sleeping together. Sleeping? They hadn't really done a whole lot of that, but it had been wonderful.

They'd gone to Tightly Bound last night. Byron had been there, but not Taylor. He'd shown them around and even gave them a tour of his own private play room. Sin had tried not to be embarrassed, but it had been difficult. Most of the "toys" he'd shown them were things she'd only heard of, not seen. Payton had asked all kinds of questions and then had spent a small fortune in the shop even with the "family" discount Byron had insisted on giving them.

But they'd used some of the things and, as it was right now, she wanted to rub her nipples where they still ached a bit from the rings he'd clamped there. She looked over at him and blushed when he winked as if he knew what she'd been thinking. She turned to David and Sally. "And I'm supposed to trust her why?" She pointed to the girl.

"Her I don't know from Adam and the last time I heard, you're still a part of my problem, not the solution."

David looked over at the girl and nodded. Something was going on and she was sure she wasn't going to like it. Blindly she reached for David's hand and he took it. Sally stood up and sat next to David.

"My name is Sally Patterson. David is…he's my dad. I'm pretty sure you can trust me as much as you do him, Miss Waite. Or do you still go by captain?"

"Mostly Sin. He calls me Sydney." She pointed at Payton with her free hand. "Daughter? I can see your mom in you. How come…you wanted to keep her safe in case? You are a sly bastard, aren't you?"

David laughed. "Her mother did it mostly. She made sure no one in the service knew about her. By the time I'd met you it had become habit and she was already away at college by then. She…she has wanted to meet you for years. I just…things went from bad to worse when you got hurt."

Sin didn't say anything. What could she say really? He was right and they both knew it. She looked over at Payton. He leaned forward and spoke to David.

"What do you mean someone is trying to kill her? Is it because of me?" Payton grinned. "You should be a little more selective about who you have investigating me. My mom has plenty of friends in high places."

David laughed. "No, though you should know that you're involved too. And when you showed up here today I figured you knew. This does have to do with you as well, as I've said. You both know a man that is indirectly and directly involved."

"Carl Wickett. Yeah, Payton told me. And he was married to my sister Quinn for about ten minutes. But what does that have to do with me? I didn't marry him…had I have, he'd be dickless about now," Sin said as she stood. "In fact, I don't think I've ever met the ass."

"I'm not really sure, but my sources tell me that he was a part of you getting attacked. He is said to have been willing to pay a bonus to the man who killed you." David handed her another file. "There was a leak in your unit. I have a man looking into it and he's pretty sure that he knows who the man is. He won't tell me. He said that he's going to take him out himself."

Sin immediately thought of Shipley. It sounded just like something he'd do. Not give her up, but take out a man he thought would be a leak.

"And you're okay with this?" Sin snorted. "You got pissy with me when I told you I wanted to knock that guy on his ass for making me wear a jock strap and you're going to let this guy kill another man on the assumption he was a leak?"

"Waite, that man was a four-star general and you said you were going to cut his balls off and use them to fill your strap, not knock him down. I believed you…still believe you as a matter of fact, but that doesn't negate the fact that he was a general and you were going against orders." David grinned at her. "I think you made your point anyway, if I remember correctly."

"What did you do?" Payton asked when Sally started laughing. "You didn't threaten the man, did you?"

"No." David was laughing so hard he could barely speak. "She convinced all the men in her squad to wear a bra filled with water balloons. All of them. And a few of them started leaking down the—" David took a deep breath before he could continue. "Down the front of their shirts and into their pants. They all looked like they'd been lactating. And they…and they had their straps on the outside of their pants just as she did."

Sin continued the story. "When the general asked me what the fuck I was doing. I told him that I wanted to make sure that my men were properly dressed and since I had to wear a strap, then it was only fair they would be required to wear a bra. When he asked me why they were wearing their undergarments on the outside I told him that it was against Army policy for me to check their clothing and I needed to make sure they were dressed for inspection."

"She got ten days in the brig and the respect of every man on that base. The general retired the following month. Said it was no longer a man's Army and he just simply wasn't going to stand for it anymore." David wiped his eyes and looked over at her. "Waite, you have any idea who I have looking into this?"

She nodded. "Shipley. He'd be the only one you'd trust after the field. He told me he was coming out to do some work. And…I saw him follow me here. I didn't know it was him until you handed me this file. Why Wickett and what do you know?"

"Actually, I was hoping you two could help me with that. He had a huge influx of money about eighteen months ago and some more over the past few months. Not a lot, but enough for us to know that he's being funded by someone with cash. The hit on your team wasn't just him…there were others higher up involved." Sin looked at Payton while David continued. "The string keeps leading higher and higher, but I'm nowhere near being done."

"David, you should back off. It's only going to get you into trouble and we both know you have more riding on this than I do. I'm out and you are still a bit from retiring." She kneeled down in front of him. "Please, for me? Back off?"

"I'm sorry, honey, but I can't. If I had done something in the weeks before you were hurt then I might have prevented it. But I didn't and you were. I'm sorrier about that than you'll ever know." David looked at Payton. "I'm expecting you to help me keep her safe. She's a bit of a hot head when she thinks she's helping someone off their asses."

Sin turned and looked at Payton to see what he'd say. He looked at her when he answered David. "We have an agreement. She is much more knowledgeable about this thing as I am in other parts of our lives. Besides, if you know her half as well as I think you do, then telling her not to do something is just like telling her to go full steam ahead."

David laughed. "I guess you do love her then. All right then. We'll keep you posted. Come on, Sally."

David stood up. Sin couldn't move. She kept looking at Payton. Love? No one said a thing about love. She opened her mouth to say something and Payton shook his head. She was still kneeling in front of the chair when Payton sat down in it.

"You keep looking at me like that and I'm going to think about ways of making use of your current position."

He lifted her chin. "They're gone. Would you like to play with me?"

She nodded. "But he said that—" The kiss was soft and thorough. She moved into it much like she would a room, fully and without reservation. Before she knew it she was up on his lap and he had her shirt unbuttoned.

~~~

Payton wasn't ready to tell her he did love her. He didn't know why, but he was sure as soon as he did she'd run. He was also sure that while she might love him, she was also terrified of it. He thought maybe he'd let her get used to him slowly. But right now…right now, he needed her.

Last night they'd gone to the club and when they'd gotten back to the house they'd played with a few of the things he'd picked up for them. There was the nipple clamps that she was currently wearing and then there was the vibrator that they'd used a great deal before she'd fallen into a dead sleep. Coop wanted to see what the clamps had done for her nipples, but wanted to be home when he did. For now he wanted to taste them.

"Feed me your breasts. I want you to lift them up and let me just suckle at them. Tell me if it hurts or not." He watched her unsnap the front closure on her black bra and slide the lace away. "You look delicious baby, good enough to eat. Do you remember what I told you last night?"

She nodded. They'd gone over the basic rules he wanted her to be aware of and some of the things he'd like to do with her. She had been a little reluctant at first, but the more he explained how it worked, the more relaxed she'd become about it. They'd ended up with her on her knees and him taking her from behind before they'd gotten too far.

"I'm going to need you to be ready to take me whenever I want. Do you understand what that means? Whenever, slave. However." She nodded again and he had to shift or hurt himself. "You may speak."

"How would you like me? If it pleases you, I'd like to take you into my mouth and suck you until you come." Her voice was soft and full of need. "Master."

Coop knew she was only learning her role and didn't know she couldn't suggest anything, but right now the thought of her taking him into her mouth nearly had him coming right then. He took her nipple into his mouth and bit just around the ring. She arched up into his mouth and moaned.

"The door isn't locked and we're not going to lock it. You'll have to hurry and make me come quickly before someone comes in or I will let them fuck you. Get on your knees and make me come." She scrambled to the floor and he stopped her by holding his larger hands over hers when she started to remove his belt. "No, through the opening. Take me now and hurry, but don't think I'm going to make it easy on you."

He was lying and he was sure she knew it. He was so ready to come he was sweating. Long lines of it were running down his back and down his ass. When she opened his zipper and pulled him free he had to bite his tongue to keep from moaning.

Her mouth covered just the head. And when her tongue began to lap along the eye of his cock he leaned back and watched her. Her head bobbed up and down and she nearly took all of his length into her mouth by swallowing hard when he got to her throat. Damn, he wasn't going to make it.

When she slid her hand beneath his ass he thought she was pulling him forward, but she nearly made him cry out when she began working her fingers to his tight hole and began rubbing the seam of his pants against it. He moved to pull his jeans down, suddenly needing to feel her there.

"That's it baby. Take me. Swallow again, let me—Christ!" Her finger punched through the tight rings as soon as his pants were down around his thighs. In and out she fucked him until he could feel his balls tightening, his climax coming quicker now, and he didn't think he'd be able to stop it, not even sure he wanted to.

When he felt the first spurt of cum hit the back of her throat he pulled out and watched it hit her face. Even as she stuck out her tongue to catch the streams of his hot juices she fucked his ass and pumped his cock. Wrapping his hand around hers on his cock he jettisoned harder on her, covering her with his cream and saying her name over and over. When he was sated she sat back on her heels and looked at him, not touching the cream dripping off of her.

"Did you come?" She shook her head no. "Do you want to?"

"Yes, master. I would like that very much." She didn't move and neither did he.

He began pumping his cock again, still semi-hard. He looked at the cum on her chin and imagined her taking him again. She was a wonder to him, in all her need to control, to give it up so readily to him during sex.

"Stand up and turn around. I want you to bend over and fuck my pretty pussy while I watch you. Come twice and I'll let you ride me until I come again inside of you. If you fake it, I'll know."

She lifted the denim skirt she had on and he nearly did come again seeing she had no panties on. The clamp he'd put on her clit had her swollen and he could see her juices trickling down her legs. He knew he wasn't going to make it. Not now.

"I've changed my mind. Turn around and ride me now. But I want your breasts unfettered. Hurry."

She took off her blouse and her bra the rest of the way and started to slip off the skirt while he watched. She was soon standing before him naked and he had never seen a more beautiful sight. When she sat on his thighs, her knees on either side of him, he reached forward and pulled her down on his cock quickly. She threw back her head and moaned.

"Ride me. Hard. I want to feel your pussy tighten around me when you come. Christ, you're killing me."

She didn't waste any time in doing what he said and her body slammed against his with enough force to make his ass slam back against the back. When he gripped her hips and showed her how to pleasure herself she came, shattered around him and milked his cock hard. Coop came with her and bit her nipple again when he felt her come down. Her second climax had her scream and he covered his mouth with hers to quiet her.

Afterwards neither of them moved. Coop was sure if anyone came in the door they wouldn't be able to even cover themselves, but would simply lay there as the newcomers looked their fill. He chuckled at that and she lifted her head from his shoulder to look at him.

"I was thinking how bad we'd look if someone came in right now. We should be more careful of that." He pulled her lax body to his. "But this feeling is much too nice to quit right now to lock it."

"It's locked," she told him as she laid her head back to his shoulder. "David locked it on the way out. It's a habit he has, locking doors when he leaves a room. It's one of the most irritating habits he has, used to drive his wife nuts."

Coop didn't know whether to be happy it was locked or happy because she knew and still played with him when he didn't. He lifted her head from his shoulder and looked at her. "Sydney, I am in love with you. You should know that now. I don't expect you to tell me you love me in return, but I do love you."

She pulled her chin from his hand and laid her head back on his shoulder. "I don't know what I feel for you," she said in his neck. "I feel something, but love...I don't know. I'm sorry."

He couldn't be sorry, not when she said she felt something for him. He pulled her closer and held her. Life would never be dull again, that was for sure. He hated to make her move, but he was getting sore again. Coop had to smile. He'd gotten more exercise in the past few days than he had the entire time he'd been in the hospital. And he was looking forward to it more and more.

They left the building and, this time, he was more alert for tails. He found the one she'd mentioned in the office.

Not too far away, but just enough to make him aware they weren't alone.

"Shipley will protect us before he'd hurt me. He was the only man I trusted inside." He glanced over at her as he drove. "I'd swear on it with my life."

He hoped it wouldn't come to that.

~Chapter 14~

Carl closed his phone and sat back in his chair. Things were progressing, but not the way he'd hoped. Shipley was doing his part, but not quickly enough, neither was he giving the information Carl wanted. Completely not his fault, but Carl needed someone to blame and he didn't care who it was.

Quinn had remarried. That was a complete surprise. He'd expected…hoped really, that he'd broken her of that. Grinning, he got up and walked to the large window that faced the back lot. She had been a lot of fun to knock around. And knowing that her big, bad-assed twin had not done a thing about it had made it more delicious for him. Until that bitch had come along.

The dyke Army bitch. He hadn't even known about her until he'd done a little investigating when he'd moved to Jersey. Sydney, the baby bitch, had taken his wife from him and had made her fight him. Him! No one fought Carl Marshall Wickett and walked away. Especially now and especially when he had made his claim. He'd been stupid to leave, not run away like they all thought, but leave.

He'd make sure both of them paid. Carl opened the door, walked out into the brisk night, and stood on the deck.

But first he'd have to stop Cooperider. Shipley had said he was in Ohio. The same small podunk town his wife was in. Carl wondered if they knew each other or if it was just a serendipity chance that they lived there. No, couldn't be. Something made him think they'd been against him all the time. Carl snorted.

He didn't like sounding like one of those paranoid pricks that thought that every cocksucker in the world was against him. He didn't actually believe that Cooperider and Quinn had set out to try and make him look bad, but he couldn't help thinking about them together now, laughing at him behind his back. When he heard his phone on the desk ring he glanced down at his watch. Only three people had this number and one of them was dead. Carl went back inside.

"This had better be good if you're calling me at four in the morning, James. And I do mean good." Carl sat behind the desk and toyed with the idea of making this man a thing of the past as well.

"The trial has been moved up three months. The prosecution has decided that you are still a flight risk and that delaying it any longer will just give you more time to flee." Dean James, his lawyer, had just gone from an idea of a dead man to an actuality. "The trial is set for next Thursday at nine in the morning."

"And you couldn't convince them for the eight hundred dollars an hour that I pay you that not only do they have my passport, my plane grounded, and my assets frozen that there is no way in hell I can run? What good are you anyway?" Carl reached into his second drawer, pulled out his gun, and laid it on the desk. "I haven't had time to make arrangements on my other little problem yet. You have to go back to them and tell them that I'm staying put in this little hovel they've reduced me to."

"I got it scheduled for next Thursday and not today. If the judge had his way you'd be in jail and not that 'hovel' you call it now. He's convinced you are living in the lap of luxury and not scraping by as I've claimed you are."

James sounded pissed and that pissed off Carl. "You think I'm living in the lap here, James? While my home in town has all the things I want and need, I sit here in the three-bedroom house with barely enough room for me much less the five servants I have running around here. This fucking sucks. Take care of this or, so help me, I will. Do I make myself understood?" Carl waited for the groveling, but was sorely disappointed in James.

"Are you threatening me?" There was a snort of laughter. "Bring it on, ass wipe, and we'll see how quickly you go from that massive house you're in to an eight-by-eight cell in minutes. Fuck you, Mr. Wickett. I quit."

The phone slammed down so hard that Carl jerked the receiver from his ear. Carl closed his eyes and started to count, but was much too pissed and way too fucking scared to do more than three numbers before he threw the entire phone across the room and hit the large glass door he'd just came in. Lucky for him...or James, that it was bulletproof or he'd have another mess to have dealt with. Carl started pacing the room.

What did his lawyer know? Everything. And that meant he had to go. Ballsy moves did not mean smart ones and Carl didn't even care to appreciate the fact that someone had stood up to him. Carl started for his desk to call someone to take care of the fucking lawyer when he remembered the phone was now in pieces on the floor. Instead, he picked up a pen and started making notes.

The second order of business was to find out why Shipley had had to kill Louis. Hartman Louis had been with Carl for years and all of a sudden he got it in his head to take out one of his workers? It didn't sound true. He tried to think what might have provoked Shipley to lie. Nothing.

Carl thought back over the past three years. Okay, there was any number of men Louis had claimed had disappeared. There was that hit man he'd hired named…well, he couldn't be expected to remember everyone's name, but he'd been found a few weeks after Louis had told him he had disappeared. Washed up on the beach, a neat hole in his forehead. The more Carl tried to think, the more nameless bodies would flitter through his memory. And all of them men that Louis had claimed hadn't worked out or had simply disappeared. Carl did laugh now. Things, he supposed, where not as pretty as Louis had made them appear.

"Well, well, you little cocksucker, met your match in Shipley, didn't you?" Carl was still laughing when his cell phone rang.

"I guess you haven't heard the good news then, have you? Your trial date has been moved. Seems you have to be back here in a few days to stand trial for the list of shit that Officer Cooperider had on you."

Carl didn't like that the mayor was saying "his stuff," as if he'd had nothing to do with it. "Yeah. James just called to inform me. He said he worked to get it until then. What's your take on this judge? Can he be persuaded?" Carl didn't like having this type of conversation on a cell, but this particular phone was supposed to be the most secure. "I don't need this shit right at the moment."

"No, he can't. Cooperider's mother is convinced that you'll go after her baby boy again and she wants you behind bars." The mayor laughed. "Not that it'll stop you once you find the prick, but it was nice of her to think you were so stupid you couldn't reach beyond this."

Carl had a sudden thought. This conversation was being recorded. First of all, the mayor never called him this early and secondly...why was he using names? "What about you getting the judge to look the other way like you did before? You remember when we needed that building inspector put on another project? You didn't seem to have any issues with the judge back then."

There was a long pause. Carl sat up in his chair and waited. He knew he was right by the mayor's next statement.

"I'm sure I don't know what you're referring to. I have to go. I've got...there's someone at the door." The line went dead.

Carl sat back. Fuck. The mayor had to go. There was no way to get around it. He pulled out his book and looked up a number then started to dial it. Before he got three numbers in he closed his phone. He couldn't take the chance. Standing up, he went to the door and then out to the garage. He wasn't sure what to think when he noticed a van pull away from the curb just as he left his drive. Carl decided that it was time to disappear. When he stopped at a light he reached over into his glove compartment and pulled out the large envelope. Dumping it on the seat beside him, he dug through it as he drove until he came up with the cell phone. Flipping it on, he waited and thought.

Shipley was his best bet now. Not only had the man kept him informed, but had taken care of a problem he'd not even known he had until then. When the phone signaled it was on he dialed the first number programmed in it.

"It's me. Be ready. I'll be there in ten," he said as soon as the call was answered. There was no greeting, just a bell sounding.

"Yes, sir." And the line went dead.

Carl smiled as he pressed the second number in the phone. "I need it all. Now. How soon?" The same type of greeting, but a different tone this time. There was a pause before anyone responded, but he was expecting this. This person had a great deal more to accomplish.

"Five hours. The usual?" the voice asked.

"Plus a ten. I need it sooner." He really didn't, but he liked it when things were on his time frame and not someone else's. He liked that people bowed down before him and scrambled to do what he wanted.

"Three and a one." The line went dead. Laughing, Carl threw the phone in the back seat and thought about what he'd gotten with less than two minutes on the phone.

The first call had been about his plane and identification to go with a trip. Not the one they knew about, but the one he had in a little port called Zanesville

Air in Zanesville, Ohio. He'd put it there several years ago and had only recently been having the pilot on standby. The ID was expensive, but he'd be a new man in a few hours. Complete with birth certificate, drivers license, and even a few credit cards. The second call was for his cash.

The person at the other end had a list of things to sell as Carl needed them. But Carl needed it all gone. A man who was in as much trouble as he was wouldn't be returning. So selling it all off was the only route to go. The greedy bastard at the other end was going to charge him another one percent to sell it all in the time he'd given him, but Carl was still going to be a very wealthy man. The extra ten he'd asked for was ten grand in immediate cash, clean and in small bills. This money would get him to his next stop.

~~~

Sin was running when her phone went off. She didn't stop, but did slow enough to look at the caller ID before deciding to answer. She smiled when she heard her brother talking to who Sin assumed was his wife.

"…said it was going to be another hour. I don't have an hour. I want to know now."

"You'd think that a man who was a doctor would have a bit more patience than you seem to have. Why is that, I wonder?" She moved the headphones from her music to her phone so she could finish her run and talk. "Couldn't you just wait the hour and then call and get the information you want?"

"No," he laughed. "Because then I wouldn't have it before I had to go to work. I like to have all my eggs in a basket before I make plans."

Sin snorted as she crossed the street. "You just like having your own way, admit it." She slowed when she noticed a light on in Mrs. Carson's house. "Alyssa should learn to tell you no more often. I'll have to give her a few lessons on that."

Mrs. Carson came out of the house just as Sin was about to go to the other side of the street. She wasn't afraid of the neighbor. He'd been in jail last she'd heard and wasn't going to be getting out anytime soon. He'd wanted Mrs. Carson to sign over her Social Security check and was pissed when she wouldn't do it. Some people didn't deserve to live.

"My wife does not need lessons on telling me no. But...I need a favor from you. Not big and if you say no, I'll understand completely. I'm only letting you live in my house for free, letting you use the car, and even giving you the space you needed even though you broke—"

"What the fuck do you want, Cain? And I offered to pay you rent and to even purchase the stupid thing from you. As for the car, I haven't used it." She grinned when she thought of pissing him off. "Who the hell would want to be caught dead in a nineteen-sixty-nine mustang when the new ones are so much cooler?"

He sputtered for a few minutes. She was glad that she'd muted her phone and he couldn't hear her laughing. Some days with Cain and his car it was like reeling him in hook, line, and sinker.

"I'll have you know that some people, men, would give their left nut for that car. Have you even gone out and looked at it? It's in prime condition. It even has the original leather seat and the radio works." He sputtered again. "You should be horse whipped for thinking…Alyssa, I didn't say I was going to… It is not just a car. Damn it, Sin, see what you started."

She unmuted the phone and let him hear her laughter. "I know, Cain, I was kidding. Is Alyssa pissed at you?"

"She thinks I should bend you over my knee and beat your ass is what she thinks. Hang on."

He put her on hold and then suddenly Alyssa was there. "Hello, Sin. What my stupid macho husband called for was to see if you'd watch Connor for us tonight. I have this dinner thing and it should only be about…"

Sin stopped listening and leaned down to catch her breath. She could hear her talking, even make out a few of the sounds, but nothing past the pounding of her heart in her head. She was almost in the house so she sat down on the step and put her head between her knees. Payton was suddenly there and she looked up at him.

"She wants me to watch Connor," she said as she shoved the phone at him and took off inside the house. Payton followed her in.

"Yes, she needed to go to the bathroom." Payton was looking at her as he held the phone to his ear. "Sure, let me have her call you back. I don't know what she has plans for, but…why don't I have her call you back? All right then, sure."

Payton didn't say anything as she stood there. She could feel the tears, but refused to brush them away.

"You going to watch him? Sounds like fun." She could only stare at him. "How old is the little guy anyway?"

"I guess he's almost one. And I can't watch him...I don't know shit about kids and it...it hurts to think about him..." She backed up when he stepped toward her. "I'll call her back and tell her I can't do it."

"Is he walking?" He took another step toward her. "You don't talk much about your family. Come to think about it, the only ones I've met are your brother Cain and Jasmine in passing. Why is that?"

"Quinn is Cain's twin; she has a set of triplets. She's married to Drew Miller. Jazzie lives in the big house, Gracie designs clothes—stop moving toward me, damn it," she snapped.

His grin pissed her off. "Why? I want to touch you. I love touching you. Tell me about the babies. Are they cute?"

She forgot how to breathe when he touched his lips to her neck. "I don't...please stop, Payton. I can't think when you do that. I've never seen the babies. I'm...I asked them to stay away. They were driving me crazy with their constant questions every day."

He pulled his mouth away, but didn't stop touching her. "You've never seen your nephews and niece? Why?" He let her go and stepped back. "Because you're afraid? That doesn't sound like you."

She glared at him. "I am not afraid. I just...I don't know any of them. I left home when I was seventeen and didn't come back much. They changed. I've changed. And for kids? I told you I don't know anything about them. I've never even held one before I held little Connor, and all he did was scream for the whole bloody time. What the hell am I supposed to do if it cries again?"

He shrugged before answering her. "Give him whatever he wants." He stared for several seconds. "So you'll watch him, right?"

~Chapter 15~

Coop watched Sin with Connor. He wasn't sure which of them was having the most fun, her or him. Right now she was "sharing" a cookie with him and his belly laughs were making them all laugh.

It had been a little touchy at first. Connor seemed to know his aunt was terrified of him and the little guy had wanted nothing to do with her. When Coop had picked the crying baby up he stopped crying and Sydney burst into tears. Coop put Connor down on the floor again when he struggled.

The little charmer had toddled over to his toys, picked up his teddy bear, took it to Sydney, and handed it to her. She hugged him and that was all there was to it.

"Give Uncle Coop some now. Aunt Sin is all filled up." Sin laughed when Connor pouted. "You look just like your daddy when you do that."

Connor had sat down on Coop's lap and started gibbering a mile a minute, gesturing his hands, and cookie crumbs went everywhere. Sin watched his every move.

"How do you know so much about kids?" she asked him. "I mean, you don't have any, do you?"

He laughed. "No. But I had a partner who had three. He'd have me over to his house a couple times a month and you tend to learn quickly what to do." He watched Connor drive his truck up and down his leg. "You did great, Sydney. He loves you already. Tomorrow night, you'll be able to watch the triplets."

"No and he...heck no. One at a time for awhile." She started picking up the toys and putting them back in the bag Alyssa had dropped off. "What kind of kids do you want to have someday?"

He started to answer, but was interrupted by the door bell. Sydney jumped up and ran to answer it. It was her brother and Alyssa.

Connor was happy to see his parents and was still going on and on with them as he rubbed his eyes. He was sound asleep on his daddy's shoulder as they left an hour later. It was well after midnight when Sydney and he went to their room. She seemed to be very nervous and confirmed it when she told him she was going to take a bath.

"If you want to just go to sleep, I promise I won't wake you." She shut the door to the bathroom quickly before he got a chance to say anything.

He knew what she was upset about. Her question. She knew he wanted children. She just wasn't aware that he wanted them with her. He loved her, he thought he had since the moment he'd seen her snarling ass in the hospital. Without bothering to knock, he went to the door and opened it.

"Did you want something? I can leave if you need to use the bathroom." She wouldn't look at him.

The water was running, but he was sure she wasn't aware she was pouring shampoo in the water instead of bath bubbles. He reached over, took the bottle from her, and turned off the taps. "I thought I'd join you. It might do my leg some good to have a nice, warm bath for a change." She nodded, stood up, and started toward the door. "No, Sydney, I want you to join me. Don't leave me to bathe alone."

With her back still toward him she whispered, "I'm really not in the mood tonight. Maybe tomorrow or something. I'm really tired."

He walked up behind her, reached around her, and unbuttoned her blouse while he spoke to her. "I can bathe with you without sex, love. I just wanted to relax with you. Come on, please? I want to sit in a tub with bubbles with you."

She nodded, but put her hands over his. "Payton, we have to end this soon. Before it's too...I think it's already too late. I can't do this anymore. I've fallen...I'm in love with you."

He turned her around. "Oh, baby, I love you too. Every prickly bit of you." Coop pulled her into his arms and held her to him. He felt her crying, but didn't say anything. She was hurting, he knew that. He even knew why. So when she spoke next, he wasn't even surprised by what she said.

"I can't be in love with you. You need to find a normal woman to love you. A normal woman who can give you those babies you said you wanted, the ones with the blue eyes and dark hair. We need to stop this after tonight, okay?" She looked up at him and his heart broke for all that she thought was wrong with her.

"Oh, Sydney, you're the only woman I want to have babies with. And even if our children have orange eyes and purple hair, I could care less as long as I raise them with you. I love you, Sydney Valeria Waite. Will you please marry me and have babies with me?"

"Payton, I can't have—"

He kissed her. It was meant to shut her up, quiet whatever else spilled from her lips, but when she growled deep in her chest, he pulled back and looked at her.

Coop laughed. "Did you just growl at me?"

"You never let me finish anything. I was going to tell you that I can't raise anything with you. I can't have children. Don't you understand what that means? No babies, no one to call your own. I'm damaged goods. I'm worthless as a mate."

He looked at her when she tried to get away and simply held her tighter. When she glared at him, he raised a brow at her until she stopped. He was sure she could have gotten away, but he was happy when she didn't.

"If you are quite finished putting yourself down I'd like a word or two myself. I don't care about your inability to have a child, Sydney. I love you just the way you are…okay, I'd like for you to be less macho, but I love that about you too. It's not having the babies I care about. Any moron can have them. It's the fact that you can be their mother that I want. You are going to be a wonderful, loving, fun mother. I mean, look at it this way. How many mothers can tell their children that they've been to the hells of the earth and survived? How many can say that their mommy has been pinned by the President of the United States and from a hospital bed? Not many, I bet. I love you, Sydney, not your womb, not your ovaries, you."

She laughed up at him. "Wow, you are a charmer, aren't you?" She laid her head on his chest and he held her. She didn't say anything for a long time. "Are you sure about this?"

"I've never been more sure of anything in my entire life. I love you and want to marry you as soon as humanly possible." He grinned. "Of course, there is this one thing…"

She looked up at him, pissed off again. "What now? You have ten other wives you've charmed with you silver tongue, haven't you? Damn it, Payton, stop laughing at me."

"We still have to tell my mom."

~~~

Damn it, she wasn't home. Carl moved through the house quietly and decided that he'd wait for her. Everything he needed was in place, but he needed this one more element to finish things off before he was going to disappear for good. He sat in the overstuffed chair in the living room and looked around.

It was a nice house. Very expensive both in furniture and grounds. The room he was in had the chair he was sitting in and several more just like it. The fireplace, a gas one, wasn't on, but he could tell that it had been recently. The room was warm and comfortable feeling.

The walls were done in a light-colored wall paper. The shelves, and there were plenty of them, were filled with pictures and small and large nick-knacks. He didn't really care for all that crap, but it did give the room a nice homey feel, he supposed. Carl had been intrigued to see the photo of Cooperider's family.

Cooperrider's father had been the commanding officer of the homicide department. No wonder Cooperider had a real hard-on to be a good cop. By all accounts his father had been one of the good guys. Carl decided that he would have hated the man on sight. Grinning, he thought about the other rooms that he'd looked into when he'd been looking for mommy dearest.

He wondered if, after this was over, he could get a good deal on it. Then he laughed. He wouldn't be in any house in the States for a long time, if ever again. This was his last big job, he'd decided…well, at least until someone else pissed him off enough where he had to kill them. He could certainly live in the lap of luxury once he landed in Belize.

He had just over ninety thousand in cash on the plane. There were several credit cards all with bogus addresses and people. His new identity was perfect and he was already trying to get used to the name. Paul Householder, he liked the sound of it. He'd put a contract out on the mayor. Shipley had come through on that little bit for him not an hour ago. And Hartman James was going to be dead by morning. Life would be perfect as soon as he could take care of his little problem with Cooperider.

He frowned when he thought of Quinn. His contract on her had been a bust and the person who had hired him to kill her wasn't all that thrilled about him having to abort the project with her. She was a devil and he was actually happy to be rid of her. He thought of her anger when he'd told her that their deal was off.

"What do you mean the water is too hot for you? You and I had a deal, you little cocksucker. You do it now or I tell the world what you've been up to since you left Ohio."

She would bring that up. "I told you before, I have no cover for this. If I take her out, then the world will be looking for me, not you. I won't be a party to this with you any longer. Everything you've planned so far has gone to shit anyway. Not one thing you've tried as—"

"And you think that's my fault?" she screamed at him. "I can't help it if you continue to fuck up by hiring the wrong group of…that last man had her in his sights. All he had to do was kill her and he froze. What the fuck am I paying you for if you can't do a simple thing and kill one defenseless woman already injured in a car accident?"

"Defenseless? You know as well as I do there was another person in that vehicle and he had a fucking gun. And on top of that, you want me to wait on my payment. Do you think men are going to wait around on you to get what you feel is coming to you? I have expenses and you, my dear lady, have paid me nothing."

She snorted. "You didn't even have to pay that last man. And if you did, you're stupider than I thought you were from the beginning. He's dead, as is every one of the hired men you've gotten to fuck up my plans. We will work together on this, Carl, or so help me there won't be a place deep enough for you to hide in."

The phone had slammed down so hard he pulled the phone from his ear. Carl was getting sick and tired of people hanging up on him. He opened his eyes when he heard a car pull into the driveway. Smiling, he stood up and walked to the door, pulling out his gun as he went.

If this didn't bring Cooperider running then nothing would. He just hoped the old broad had a way to contact her little boy or he wasn't sure what to do. He hid behind the large vase in the entrance hall and waited. This was going to be so easy; he wondered why he hadn't thought of it sooner.

A guard entered first. Carl had been expecting this and waited until the woman came in too. She was dressed up in a nice dress and him in a tux. Carl wondered for a second if he could fence her jewels and decided he would strip her of them as soon as he got her on his plane. When she turned to shut the door Carl shot the man in the head and turned the gun on to Candace Cooperider.

"Don't do it," he told her when she reached for the alarm button on the wall. "I've already disabled your security system and calling the cops now will only get you dead. Where's your son?"

"Payton? How should I know? He's a grown man and—"

He backhanded her with the gun. When she crumpled to the floor he realized he probably shouldn't have hit her so hard. She was a tiny thing for having such a big kid and he wondered if maybe Cooperider was adopted. He was searching her bag for weapons when he heard a voice down the hall.

"Mom, is that you? I thought you would be a little— Who are you?" Carl smiled at the woman. "What have you done to my mom?"

"I'm taking the two of you with me. Didn't know Cooperider had a little sister. Might have a bit more fun than I first thought. No you don't." He fired at her feet when she started to turn and run. "You get your ass over here and sit down. Tell me where your brother is and I might leave your mommy here and only take you."

"Payton? I don't know. He only calls Mom. She has a cell she is supposed to call him on if she needs him. Don't hurt my mom, please?"

Carl made a decision to take both women. Two for the price of one, so to speak. When he had the brother he'd take the little sister and have some fun with her before he killed her too. It would be delicious knowing that she was Cooperider's sister and he was going to make sure that he knew everything he was going to do to her before he killed him too.

Getting the women to the plane proved to be more difficult than he'd thought it should have been. He'd finally had to threaten the daughter with the gun before the mother came along peacefully. Carl didn't want to kill the girl, but he had no problem hurting her a bit. It had only taken a broken arm to get the mother to cave on his demands. He'd wanted her to fight more, but she didn't. Once they were on the plane and headed to Ohio he told them what he wanted.

"You are going to contact your son. And once I get in touch with him I will let you both go." He tried for a reassuring smile, but the mother saw right through it.

"You mean you're going to kill us after you find my son, then kill him too. I know who you are, you piece of shit. You're that cop Wickett. Well, buster, I'm not going to play that game. You let my daughter go and I'll tell you where Payton is."

Carl hit the girl again. "You'll tell me now or, so help me, I'll have her tossed from this plane. I don't give two shits about either of you. It's that son of a bitch son of yours I want. He's cost me a great deal and I plan to collect."

In the end he'd had to shoot the girl in the leg before the mother decided to play by his rules. Her threat of Payton tearing him limb from limb didn't bother Carl. He figured he had the upper hand in that he had the boy's mother. Nobody fucked with somebody's mother, even he knew that. Plus, and this was the biggest thing of all, Cooperider didn't have a clue that he had his mother and that he was currently on his way to find him. He was going to have fun with this and he couldn't wait to see the man's face when he shot his mommy in the head before Carl killed him.

~Chapter 16~

Her phone was ringing. Sin tried to remember where she'd put it when Payton rolled over her and handed it to her. With a quick kiss he rolled back over and went back to sleep. She looked at the caller ID and nearly fell off the bed in her need to answer it. She didn't even get out a greeting before he barked an order to her.

"Kitchen. I'm waiting." Then the line went dead.

Sin pulled on some clothes then woke Payton. She had no idea why, but she wanted him close. She started out the door, but turned and retrieved her gun from under the pillow and checked the magazine before she looked up at Payton.

"Do you think you'll need that?" he asked as he pulled on a pair of jeans.

Her mouth watered at the sight of all that flesh, but she turned her back to him so she could think. "I don't know. But I'd rather be armed than not." She watched as he did the same and slipped his gun in the back of his jeans. "Thank you."

"No problem. We are an odd couple and I can live with that." With a quick kiss to her nose they went down the stairs.

They entered the kitchen with caution and looked at the man sitting at the table with a glass of iced tea and a box of donuts in front of him. The light from the moon shone on his dark clothes and bald head. Sin reached for the light switch when he stopped her.

"Don't. The less people who know we're up, the better. You Cooperider?" Payton nodded. "Good, you might as well have a seat too. This involves you more than anyone."

Sin grabbed two more glasses from the cabinet and opened the fridge. She wasn't surprised to find the light out and it dark in there as well. She put the jug of tea on the table and let Payton pour them both a glass.

"You know a man named Wickett?" Again, Payton nodded. "He's got a real hard-on to see you dead. I don't care why, but you should know he's been a busy man tonight. I've been—"

"Who the hell are you? I'm sorry, but this is a little much. We get woke up in the middle of the night, come down to a darkened kitchen to find you sitting here having breakfast as though you don't have a care in the world, and you tell me Wickett is out to get me. I know that. Do you think we can start from the beginning? I'm Payton Cooperider and you are..."

Sin grinned. "Payton, this is Roger Shipley, my friend. This is the man that David told us about. He's been working undercover, remember?"

The men shook hands before Shipley continued. "Wickett has your mother and sister. Can't tell you where he has 'em right now, but I think he might be coming here. He took them about an hour ago."

"Wait. That can't be. My mother has armed guards with her at all times. How can…he killed them. Fuck." Payton got up to pace. "You say an hour. His plane was grounded and he was being followed. I take it he has other means of transportation."

"Could be," Shipley said. "He hired me about eight months ago to do some work for him. And before you ask, I can only share what I know for sure, the rest is up to Patterson to tell you. The government thinks he had a bit to do with what went down in Africa. I'm not so sure he was the head of it, but he had been in on it. He just doesn't strike me as the planning and follow through sort of guy. Sort of a dumbass, if you ask me. Someone, maybe the governor of his state, is working with someone higher on the food chain than Wickett to get the ball moving on a few more projects. But Wickett did need you dead cause of this trial coming up."

"You told him where I was." Payton sat down hard. "I don't understand how you found me when he couldn't."

"Because he's looking for Quinn too, right?" Sin asked. She figured a man like Wickett had given up too easily when he'd run away with his tail between his legs. "And when you found Quinn, you found me, and through me, Payton."

"Something like that." Shipley grinned again. "You look good, Cap. Getting laid regular-like suits you."

"Fuck off, Shipley. You brought a killer to my door. I'm in no mood to play nice with you." She started pacing. "If he took Payton's family an hour ago, where would he be coming from?"

Payton answered first. "Virginia. My sister Shaller is living with my mom temporarily. Do you know if they are hurt?"

"No, don't know anything other than there was a dead man in the house and three more on the property. The house wasn't broken into. The alarms were disengaged so we know he was inside when she came home. There was some blood, but not enough to indicate anyone was hurt badly enough to be dead." Shipley reached into his jacket and pulled out an envelope. "Took those for you. You know that man there?"

Payton opened the envelope and several pictures spilled out. "Yeah, this man is my mother's personal guard. Phillip Salix. He had been with my dad before her." While he looked through the pictures, Sin questioned Shipley.

"What kind of transport does he have? And has he changed ID yet?" She pulled a sheet of paper off the memo tablet on the wall. "Tell me what you know and what sort of things we have to work with."

"A plane he had in Zanesville. I knew about it, but figured he couldn't get to it. Should have figured he'd have a hidey hole somewhere. Far as I can tell, he had all his worldlies sold in a few hours before he landed in Virginia. Cost him a pretty penny too. He was in and out of the house before I knew he was gone. I was on another assignment for him when he pulled that shit."

"I don't know this man. He wasn't a part of the group that regularly took care of my mom." Payton handed the picture to Shipley. "Who is he?"

"Figured someone had to let him in the house so that could be him, I suppose. Must have been part of his crew at one time or another, but nothing I can verify. He had some jerk-off tailing me for a few days, but I took care of him. Had to set him straight on a couple of things before he decided to die. Oh yeah, got a message for you. Your chief said to tell you to kill the bastard and get your ass back to Jersey. He is tired of covering your ass."

"My chief?" Payton looked hard at Shipley. "How the hell did you know about my chief and where the hell did you see him?"

"That's where I was when your mom was being taken. He, Wickett, had me go and do a few...he called them clean-ups. I had to kill the mayor and your chief. The mayor is sitting in a jail cell singing his heart out and your chief, last I saw him, was taking notes." Shipley pulled out a cell. "Said when you believed me, I was to have you call him."

Payton put the phone in his pocket without calling. Sin was grateful for his trust. "Tell me what you know about my mom and sister. Tell me like you would her." Payton pointed at her. "I want to be a part of this and get her back and make that cocksucker pay."

~~~

When his cell phone rang an hour later Coop wasn't surprised. His mom was the only one who had this number and she would only call him if it were an emergency. What he was surprised about was how long it had taken her to call. That worried him more than anything. He didn't want to think about what Wickett had been doing to them since he'd taken them. As insane as Coop thought Wickett was…he really didn't want to think about that.

"Hello, dear," his mother said. "I'm in a bit of a wicket pickle here. I was wondering if you could please meet your sister and me somewhere? We have some rather pressing issues that need to be taken care of."

Coop made notes. "Wickett has her, another male, armed." His mom was good. She'd let him know by a few phrases all that information rather quickly. She hadn't been married to a detective for all those years not to pick up that "pickle" equaled another male and "pressing" meant armed. The "wicket" part told him that Wickett did indeed have her.

"Must be bad if you're calling me this time of morning. Are you okay? Is Shaller? You're making me ner—"

"Fuck you, Cooperider." Wickett cut him off. "I have your mother and your sister here. If you don't do as I tell you, and right fucking now, I'll—"

Coop hung up when Shipley gave him the signal. "I hope you're right about this. If you get my family hurt by your tricks I will shoot you myself."

Shipley grinned a not so friendly grin. "Guy has a temper. When he's pissed off—like someone hanging up on him—the little bastard throws things. Like phones. We need him on a land line where we can trace."

When Coop's phone rang again it was his mom's number again. Coop took a deep breath and answered.

170

"You fucking hang up on me again and I'll—" Coop closed his phone on Wickett a second time when Shipley nodded.

Sydney sat in his lap and reached for his hand. He was nervous and pissed. He wanted to make demands, scream at Wickett to tell him where his mom was, but knew deep down it wouldn't get him anywhere. When his phone rang again it was a number he didn't know.

"Keep him talking. He'll wanna brag, let him. Then, when we get the address, we'll go and get your family."

Payton wasn't going with them. Sydney had explained that he had never done this before, but she and Shipley had. Plus, he had to go wherever it was that Wickett told him, to buy time and wait.

"We've worked as a team for ten years. We know each other well enough that words aren't necessary to get the job done. We do this…did this all the time. I promise you that we will do everything we can to get them out safely."

He knew she was right, but he didn't have to like it. "You'll owe me for this big time. Understand?"

Her eyes had dilated and her pulse at her throat picked up. She understood all right. She understood and wanted it as badly as he did. The phone ringing again didn't make him want her any less.

"You son of a bitch. Do you have any idea what you made me do? If you hang up on me again, I swear to Christ, I will kill your fucking mother." He was screaming through the connection. "I'm in charge. I say where and you say when. Understood?"

"Yes," Coop said as he pulled Sydney close. "I would like to speak to my family. Please. I won't...I will only meet with you if I can hear their voices."

There was a long pause. Coop knew he hadn't hung up. The timer on the little tracer was still running. The computer screen was moving all over the place trying to find the call.

"Payton, darling, don't do it. He's going to kill you and you know it," his mother sobbed in the phone.

"I know, Mom. Are you all right?"

"Yes, I'm—"

"Your sister is a bit worse for wear, but she can talk...for now," Wickett said as if he thought it was the funniest thing in the world. "So you'll have to pardon her sobbing."

"I'm going to enjoy killing you, you mother fucker." Payton watched as an address popped up on the screen in front of him. "Let me talk to my sister or it's a no deal."

Coop could still hear him laughing as Shaller spoke. "Payton? Please come and get us. He's shot me and hurt mom. Please?"

"I'm coming, baby. I'll have to take care of that piece of shit, but I'm coming for you."

"How nice of you to think you have any way of coming out ahead on this. You'll meet me at the mall parking lot in one hour. Penny's side. Come alone and unarmed and I'll tell you where to find your sister. Mommy dearest will be with me." Then the line went dead.

Coop held Sydney while no one spoke. An hour, Wickett had said. He had one hour to try and figure out how to save his mom and sister.

"Payton, we have it under control. I promise you, we do this a lot. Shipley and I—"

"How can you trust him?" he snarled at Sydney, cutting her off. "He already told you he's been working with Wickett for nearly a year. What if this is a plan to separate us and to kill us both?" Coop knew he was being unreasonable. He didn't actually believe that anyone was out to get him except for Wickett. But he was scared and pissed.

"Had I wanted you dead, Cooperider," Shipley said as he stood, "I would have shot you both while you lay upstairs naked in that big bed of yours."

"Shipley, I—"Sydney started, but was cut off by the man standing there.

"It's all right, Cap. He doesn't have any reason to trust me." Shipley opened the door. "I'm going to get the sister. You got the mom?" Sydney nodded. "Good. Meet you at the hospital in two." Then he slipped out the door.

~Chapter 17~

Sin parked her car in the accounting firm lot twenty minutes later. She saw three cars in the lot at the mall as she'd driven by, knowing one had to be Wickett's. She got out of the car and jogged to the closest bus stop.

She got on the first bus going back to the mall ten minutes later and was dropped off there in four minutes. She was just entering one of the side entrances with a group of mall walkers when her phone vibrated in her pocket. It was Shipley.

"There's a Glock twenty-three in the trash can in the ladies room near Garfield's. Three clips are taped to the lid," he told her when she answered.

She grinned. "I'm not even going to ask you how you managed that without being seen." She walked inside the bathroom. "How close are you to the hotel?"

"Ten mikes. That boyfriend...you gonna marry him?" He would ask, she thought, and knew he'd know if she lied to him. She decided to be evasive.

"He asked." She pulled out the modified Glock with the silencer and put it in the back of her pants. The one she'd brought from home was tucked in the holster at her ankle. The clips, she put into her pockets.

"Seems like a good guy." The pause was long, but she knew Shipley well enough to know he was thinking of a tactful way to ask her something. "He know?"

"Yeah." She looked up as a woman entered the bathroom. "Gotta go, Dad. See you soon."

The chuckle at the other end gave her comfort. She didn't know why, but it did. She moved out to the mall main concourse. She went to the large open area and sat down. Her phone vibrated again.

"I love you," Payton said as soon as she answered. "I'm sorry I didn't tell you before you left, but I do."

"I love you too. Where are you? And for the record, you did tell me, twice." She moved to the chair when two women sat in her view of the parking lot.

"Just pulling off Sixty. Have you heard from your buddy yet?"

Sin stood when she saw Payton's car pull in. "Just now. He's about there. Don't look for me. I'll get your mom then you can take care of the bastard. But remember what I said to do if he has her as a hostage. You have to trust me to do my part." Sin slipped out of the mall with another couple as she spoke to him. "Payton?"

"Yeah, I know. Don't move around. You are going to owe me big time for this. I'm going to want you tied to my bed for a week. And don't think that pretty ass of yours is going to not feel the slap of my belt either." She could hear him panting as hard as she was. "Christ, I want to fuck you right now."

She knew what he was doing. He was doing for both of them. Trying to get them to think about anything but what they were about to do. She, and possibly he, was going to kill someone. She was used to pulling the trigger, but he wasn't as seasoned at it as she was.

"Payton, please don't do this now. Damn it, my nipples are aching right now." She laughed when he growled. "Behave. And be safe or, so help me, I'll be the one hurting your ass in the bedroom."

His laughter was still echoing in her ears when she closed the connection. She slipped between two cars, took off her lime green jacket, and stuffed it under the car next to her to reveal her black long sleeved shirt. She pulled a black skull cap down over her face that covered her all the way to her chin. It was just after seven o'clock in the morning and just dark enough that she hoped she wouldn't be noticed.

Sin saw the doors open of the car about thirty feet away from her and an older woman stepped out. A man got out of the back seat just behind her. Sin looked at the picture again to be sure she had the right person and confirmed it was Mrs. Cooperider.

Sin waited for the next call and thought about the one she'd made to Caitlynne Grant on the way over here. She was one pissed off cop. And Sin found she kinda liked the woman for that.

"I don't like being in the dark about shit going on in my city, Miss Waite." Her voice had been barely civil and held a great deal of pissed-offness.

"You're not in the dark. I'm telling you right now. I haven't killed anyone...yet. There may or may not be a shooting in the lot of the mall and I would very much appreciate it if you'd keep your cops away in the near future."

Sin could hear the woman counting and nearly laughed at her, but caught herself. She didn't think the woman would appreciate it much and would probably order her shot on sight if she did.

"May or may not doesn't…what the fuck is going on? And why am I just now—I have someone at my door at six-thirty. Could you have anything to do with that?"

"Yes, ma'am. I thought you might like the story better coming from the one who is in charge of it." Sin was glad she'd called David first. "His name is David Patterson and he's going to explain to you what is going on."

Sin listened to the exchange between the two of them. David, ever the diplomat, was polite and cordial. Sin probably would have shot the woman or tied her up and left her there until the mission was complete. But hearing her take a strip of hide off David made her think Captain Grant would have shot first.

"All right, Waite," she said as she came back on the line. "I'm going to keep my cruisers away, but I swear to Christ, if a civilian so much as gets a hangnail from this I'm hauling your ass in on every charge I can come up with."

Sin hung up. She was only concerned about one civilian getting hurt and he was just now getting out of his car.

~~~

Coop couldn't see Sydney, which he supposed was the point. He looked at his mom then and nearly leapt toward her.

"Don't move or she's dead. Are you armed?" Wickett asked.

Coop nodded. Sydney told him to be armed and not to lie when asked. Some people would do the stupidest things when stressed and maybe Wickett was just dumb enough not to check.

"Good boy. Throw your piece toward the grassy area. Then I want you to cross your arms over your chest where I can see your fingers."

Coop took the Glock out of the back of his pants by two fingers. He glanced to his left to throw the gun and nearly bobbled it. Sydney was laying there, flat as the ground. Fuck. He tossed the gun more toward her feet and was glad when it didn't hit her.

Coop looked back at his mom. She'd been beaten. Her lip was bloodied and he could just make out her blackening eye. But she stood proudly before the man who was hiding behind her.

"You okay, Mom?"

He saw a ghost of a smile before her lip thinned out in apparent anger. "He shot your sister in the leg. I hope you know I'm not happy with you for disobeying me, young man."

"No, ma'am. I know you're not. But I have it under control." At least he hoped he did.

Wickett laughed. "How touching. You got nothing under control, you son of a bitch. Walk toward me slowly or I blow a hole in your mommy's head."

"You'll tell me why first," Coop said suddenly. He had to stall. Sydney couldn't move on Wickett until she heard from Shipley.

They weren't sure if he moved Shaller again before he'd left the hotel. And they didn't want to take the chance of her dying without medical care. Coop looked at his mother and wondered just how badly Shaller had been hurt.

"Why? You mean other than the fact that you fucked up my plans for my future? Shit, Cooperider, you've done nothing but be a goody-two-shoes since I met you." Wickett shook Coop's mom hard as he continued. "Why the fuck couldn't you have just been a rich dick and stayed out of my way? Damn it, you should have died that night. That bullet I put in your gut should have—"

"You shot my son?" Coop couldn't believe how quickly his mother turned on Wickett. "He almost died, you asshole."

"Mom," Coop tried.

"Don't you 'mom' me, Payton Riley Cooperider. I'm the one who sat next to your bed day and night while this man—"

"Shut up," Wickett said as he drew back to hit her.

Coop started forward, but Sydney was suddenly there. "Don't fucking move." Sydney had a gun to his temple as she wrapped her other arm around his throat.

Her sudden "down" had Coop lunging for his mother and pulling her beneath him. He felt something hard spray along his back. Shots were being fired. He put his hand over his mom's face.

What seemed an eternity but was probably only a few seconds, Coop heard a body drop beside him. The sun was just up enough where he could see Wickett's body lying in a pool of blood. Since he couldn't see Sydney he started to rise when she said "don't" beside his head. He'd not even heard her move.

"I think I got him," she whispered. "But I can't be sure. Call the troops. Tell Grant that there was another shooter in the CPA's office across the street from the mall. Tell her one dead bad guy. That should make her happy."

Coop turned to look at her. There was blood all over her shirt.

"It's not mine," she told him quietly.

"My daughter," his mom whispered while Coop called the number he'd been given at the house. "Is she...that hotel we were at was guarded. We have to get to her. She's been hurt badly."

"Your daughter is on the way to the hospital. A friend of mine...he made sure she was safe before he called me." Sydney moved over and put her mouth close to his when he closed the phone. "Kiss me please, Payton. I've had a shitty day so far."

He'd never been so happy to kiss anyone in his life. But it wasn't near long enough. They could hear the sirens in the background getting closer.

As they loaded his mom in the ambulance Coop tried to keep his eye on Sydney. She was talking to Captain Grant. Well, she was listening to Captain Grant. She was doing all the talking, loudly as a matter of fact. Sydney just kept grinning. Coop wasn't sure, but he thought that might have been pissing the captain off more.

"You're in love with her, aren't you, son?" his mother asked from the gurney they were latching down to the floor of the squad.

He looked back at her. "Yes, ma'am, I certainly am. And I'm going to marry her as soon as we can get a license too." He laughed when she tisked at him. "Mom, she's wonderful and I want to spend the rest of my life with her as soon as I can start it."

"I don't think you waiting for me to plan a proper wedding with her family will be that much of a hardship on you." She opened her mouth when the EMT told her to. As soon as the thermometer was gone she picked up right where she left off. "Who is her family anyway?"

Coop simply threw back his head and laughed. "Oh, you're going to love them."

~Chapter 18~

Sin listened to Captain Grant rant at her. She didn't say much back to her. She knew when to keep her mouth shut, contrary to popular belief. The woman was majorly pissed off and it didn't take a college degree to see that. But at what, Sin wasn't so sure about.

"And now I have a wounded shooter running around and I don't know where he's at and I don't have any idea how badly he's hurt."

Oh yeah, Sin thought, there was that. "By the amount of blood, I'd say not so much. He's probably holed up somewhere licking his wounds until he thinks it's safe to come out."

"And you know a great deal about blood…never mind. I don't want to know. I'm putting you on notice, young lady. If I hear you've so much as jay walked I will bring you in on charges so quickly that your head will spin."

Sin nodded. "Yes, ma'am. But I would like to say one thing if I can. Sort of need to point something out."

Cait glared and Sin tried her best not to grin. "You say something stupid and I won't be held responsible for what I do to you. You speak to your commanding officer this way? If so, then it's small wonder that he didn't—"

"She had no respect for me whatsoever," David said behind her. "She was by far the worst solider I've ever had and also the best leader. Hello again, Captain Grant."

"Hello. She is a tyrant. I have a dead cop and no way of knowing who the fuck he is because someone"—she looked pointedly at Sin—"took it into their head to use him as a shield."

Sin snorted. "I suppose you thought I should just let whoever was shooting at me kill me? Hardly. Besides, you saw what he'd done to Mrs. Cooperider. And the girl...I don't think I know her name."

"Shaller Hall. Captain Grant, David," Payton said as he came up beside her. The ambulance drove off, sirens and lights making the early morning shoppers on alert if the way they were moving about was any indication.

"As I was saying," Sin tried again. "You told me not to get a civilian killed. I didn't. I didn't even get myself hurt, much to your dismay. Instead of beating me up about this, why don't you flipping say thanks? You know what? I don't give a shit. I'm going home."

She was nearly to the car when a cop stopped her. She could have hurt him, but didn't. Her mood was just that close to the edge that she wasn't sure that she'd be able to just hurt him a little.

"What the fuck do you want?" Sin snarled at him instead. "Unless you're planning to arrest me, I would suggest you back the fuck up and get out of my way."

He swallowed twice before he spoke. "The captain…Captain Grant said that you have to come down to the station house. She said…I'm supposed to tell you she needs your fingerprints."

Sin turned back to see Payton coming toward her and the captain yelling at David. She looked back at the officer. "Tell her that she can get them from David Patterson. I've had a long night and if you try to stop me you'd better shoot me because I'm going around you or over you. It's entirely up to you."

She suddenly needed to get away. Far away, and she didn't want anyone around her right now. She started to stretch, but only got as far as bringing her hands up over her head before she felt someone push her against the car in front of her. Before she could turn on the person, she heard Payton at her ear.

"Either get in on your own or I'll put you in. I'm in no mood to fuck around with you at the moment."

"Let me go. I'm going to run and I don't want you near me." She struggled in vain to get away, but he had his body pressed completely over hers and there was no give on the car. "Get the fuck off me or so—"

His cock pressed in her ass. She felt her pussy cream up and her nipples tighten in her bra.

"I take you here or we find somewhere more private." His hot breath heated her already sensitive skin as he growled at her. "I'm too close to not caring where I am when I do it. Get in the fucking car."

She did, but not without trying to hurt him first. But before she tried again she took a good look at him. He was pissed. Not just pissed, but really pissed. She jerked away from his grip on her arm, walked to the other side of the car, and got in. Well, she thought, she wasn't any happier with him either.

They drove for about ten minutes, neither of them saying a word. When they pulled up in front of a hotel downtown she nearly said something to him, but stopped when he spoke.

"You had better be telling me that you're going to be naked as soon as we're in a room or hell will be paid. I want to fuck you so badly right now you're going to be sore for a week when I'm through."

She sat there, stunned, when he got out and went into the office. She was still sitting there when he came back and drove to the back of the lot.

"I'm not sleeping with you, you arrogant prick. I want you to take me home. I've had enough of this shit to last me two lifetimes."

Actually, she wasn't sure why she was so pissed at him. But it was boiling just there at the surface. He got out of the car and came to her side. When he wrenched the door open and pulled her out she tried to fight him, but he simply rammed his shoulder into her belly and tossed her over his shoulder. The hard smack on her ass had her seeing stars.

"You are going to pay for that, you asshole. No one beats my ass and gets—" She was suddenly airborne and bounced twice on the bed before he was on top of her. She didn't even have time to scream before his mouth was over hers.

Need exploded in her. When she felt him clawing at her clothes she tried to push his hands away and do it herself when he grabbed her hands and clamped them in his.

"Don't move. I swear to Christ. I need to do this my way. I need to…Christ, Sydney, I need to fuck you hard."

He tore at her clothes. She felt his hands pulling at her pants. When they were just open, his hand snaked into them and he plowed his fingers deep into her panties and into her slit. She nearly came off the bed.

"Fuck, you're wet. I need to be inside of you now, baby. I'm sorry, but I can't be nice right now."

He tore her bra away, took her nipple into his mouth, and bit. Screaming out his name, she began riding his finger as he sucked her nipple harder and harder. She was so close, but knew in some way that he'd punish her if she came. She struggled to get away from him and when he jerked his hand from her pussy and flipped her over onto her belly she tried to scramble away. Her jeans and panties came down quickly and he swatted her ass again. Pain and pleasure shot through her as he yanked her clothes off. When he pressed his finger over her puckered ass she stilled.

"I'm going to fuck you here soon. I'm going to ram my cock deep in this hole and fuck you raw." His voice was harsh, hard, and she felt her pussy clench at the sound. When he pulled her hips back he entered her hard. His cock slid into her pussy so fast she nearly came again.

He didn't move as she felt his cock pulse in her. His finger at her ass moved around faster now and she could feel him stretching her with small punches of his finger entering her.

"When I get you home I'm going to tie you to the bed and stretch this ass for me. I'm going to fuck this tight hole while I use that new vibrator on your pussy and feel you come. Would you like that? Would you like me to fuck you raw, Sydney?"

"Yes," she hissed. He started moving then, slow at first. When she moved back to bring more of him in her, he slapped her ass again.

"Don't move. And don't come." He draped his body over hers, his arms braced on either side of her. "I want to fuck you like this until I come inside of you. Then I'm going to fuck you again."

"Please. Please, Payton. Let me come, please."

He didn't answer her, but started pumping into her. His strokes were hard and long and when he bit her shoulder and held her still with his teeth, she knew she wasn't going to last. She clenched her pussy around him, hoping that if she could make him come he'd let her. But his growl made her stop. She was at his mercy and her body loved it.

Dizzy now, she nearly collapsed when he roared out his release. She felt him thicken in her and she could feel her own body start to go over the edge. Suddenly he pulled free of her and she whimpered. When he flipped her to her back she felt him move her legs up to his shoulders as he entered her. His strokes were slower this time, filling her with his cock as he looked down at her.

"You are mine. Say it, you're mine."

She shook her head, knowing that what he was saying…demanding something she didn't want, couldn't want.

"Tell me you belong to me and I'll let you come."

"I belong to no one. You can't keep me from coming. I'm my own person and I can fucking come if I want."

He stopped so suddenly she moaned. He held her with his hands at her calves, her feet around his neck and his cock deep inside of her. Then he pulled away and got off the bed. Her legs dropped without his support.

Neither of them said anything for a few minutes. Her breaths burned in her lungs, her need to finish made her heart pound. When he spoke low, his head was buried in his hands while his elbows rested on his thighs.

"You have no idea what it was like for me to see you lying there on that ground. You haven't a clue what it did to me to watch you drop to the ground next to me covered in blood." He glanced over at her. "You don't get it, do you?"

"Get what? That you dragged me in here and took me? That you needed to dominate me so much you wouldn't let me come until you got your jollies? Yeah, I get it. Big, bad Payton Cooperider didn't like not being in control and had to take me like I was an animal."

He stood then. His pants, she realized then, were around his thighs. "Is that what you think this was about? That I had to prove to you that I could be bigger and meaner to you?"

She sat up when he started pulling off his clothes. She wasn't sure what he thought he was doing, but if he thought she was having sex with him again, he was insane.

"Wasn't it? You didn't bite me like I was some...some fucking dog you had to fuck, like you didn't want to see my face, like I was—"

"You tell me you didn't enjoy that and I'll never do it again. Tell me you didn't get wetter because I was covering you." He waited perhaps ten seconds before he demanded again. "Tell me, damn it."

She watched as he moved toward her and the bed again. He was so close now she could see his eyes were dark, so dark purple that they looked black. But it was his cock that had her mesmerized. He was hard and full. His balls were heavy and she licked her lips at the thought of what he would taste like. When he wrapped his hand around himself she reached out, ran her thumb over the tip, and gathered the creamy pearl of him just at the slit.

"Did I hurt you, Sydney?" he asked again. "Did I hurt you when I took you like an animal?"

"Yes. Not...I want to taste you, Payton. I want to suck your cock until you come down my throat. Please?"

He kept stroking his cock, his hand going up and down in slow, tight movements. "I'm close to coming now. I could come all over your body and watch it drip off you and then you could lick me clean. I'm sorry I hurt you. And it had nothing to do with dominating you because of what you'd done. I was scared...terrified, and pissed. I'm so sorry."

He moved closer to her, his cock in front of her face, but she didn't touch him. She did open her mouth. His groan made her look up at him.

"Lay back on the bed. I want to...I need to make it up to you."

She hurried to do as he asked. And when he straddled her and pressed her breasts around his cock as he pinched her nipples, she watched as he fucked her.

"You have no idea how long I've wanted to do this. To fuck your tits this way and come on your face. Christ, you're going to kill me yet."

Sydney raised her head enough that she could lick his cock every time he got close to her mouth. He took her hands and wrapped them at her breasts, then held onto the headboard as she continued to fuck her. She wanted him to come, and she realized at the moment that she did belong to him.

~~~

He was going to come on her. It was just a matter of this second or two seconds from now. Watching her tongue slide out and taste him every time he broke through her flesh made his balls tighten more. He grabbed her head and held her up when he felt the hot grip of his climax.

The first stream hit her in the mouth and she moaned as she lapped it. Over and over he sprayed her. Her chin, her hair, he came hard and long, his cum shooting out of him in an almost painful way. When he was empty he felt her legs move beneath him.

He'd come three times and she hadn't. He felt his cock twitch, but he was spent. Moving off her he rolled around until his mouth was over her pussy. She was soaking wet; the sheet beneath her was saturated with her cream. When he pulled her nether lips open her clit was stiff and hard, ready for him to take.

The first slide of his tongue against it had her raising her hips to meet his mouth. She tasted delicious; her pussy tasted of him and her and he drove his tongue deep to take more. Sliding his hands beneath her, he started to fuck her pussy with his fingers as his other hand went beneath her and moved into her ass. She shifted his hips and, before he knew it, his cock was in her mouth and her fingers were moving along his ass. Incredibly, his cock began to stiffen.

When she entered him with her slim finger, he bit her clit. The pain/pleasure was amazing and he hoped she wouldn't stop. Soon he was fucking her mouth again and her pussy was gushing cream out almost faster than he could drink. Pulling his head up slightly he shouted for her to "come now," and she detonated around him as his cock surged again and again.

He couldn't move. He managed to roll off her, but his body refused to do much more. After a brief rest he crawled around until they were both on the pillows and he got the covers over them. Closing his eyes he thought maybe he'd never move from this spot again.

~Chapter 19~

Sin woke suddenly. She didn't move and kept her breathing low and normal. She wasn't sure what woke her, but something had. It took her several minutes of being on alert before she let her mind and body relax. Nothing.

The man next to her stirred slightly then he continued his soft snores into deeper sleep. He had his arm wrapped around her waist as he spooned against her back side. She started to close her eyes again when she felt him nip at her shoulder then roll over.

Payton had taken her and she'd loved it. It wasn't as if she was now having second thoughts about what they'd done. She'd loved every second of it. What frightened her was that she'd needed it. No, that wasn't it either, she needed him.

Sydney Waite didn't need anyone. Or she thought she didn't want to need anyone. He'd become too important, too... Fuck, she loved him.

Lifting his arm from her, she slipped out of the bed and onto the floor. She sat there and wondered what the hell she was supposed to do now. She didn't want to need him and she certainly didn't want him to need her. Not because of the sex. No, she couldn't give him what he needed. Children.

Standing, she nearly crumpled back to the floor. She was sore. Not only sore, but incredibly sore. Looking down at her bare body she could see bruises and scrapes. Not just from the rough sex, but from the incident from the mall lot as well. Gathering up her tattered clothes she went to the bathroom. She closed and locked the door before turning on the light.

Turning on the shower first, she looked at herself in the mirror. There was a bruise on her jaw and a couple of scratches on her cheek and forehead. She knew all these injuries were from the gravel parking lot. The bruises on her torso were not.

The ones at her breasts were dark and looked like fingerprints. She felt her nipples tighten when she thought of Payton taking her the way he had again. Her nipple clamps were gone and she wondered when he'd removed them. The one at her clit she knew he'd taken off before he'd tasted her.

There were bruises at her hips, more fingerprints, and a cut along her thigh. Shaking her head, she stepped into the shower and scrubbed her body hard.

She was trying to figure out what to do about her panties when her phone slipped out of her jean pocket and fell on her discarded towel.

"Fuck," she whispered. She had turned it to vibrate when she'd gone out of the mall and had forgotten it just this morning. And now it was late afternoon.

Leaving the bathroom, she had a moment of regret. She wanted to…she wanted to explain to him, but she knew that he'd convince her he didn't care, that it would work out, and she couldn't do it. She leaned down to his neck, took a deep breath of him in and, with tears in her eyes, left him. It was better for them both, she thought, and wondered which part of her was less convinced, her heart or her mind.

She was pulling out her cell phone to listen to the messages when it vibrated in her hand. She smiled when she answered, but it wasn't because she was happy.

"Can't a girl have a few hours of R&R without you bugging the shit out of her? I mean—"

"I'm shot. Come…you have to come to me. I'm…he's getting away."

Sin rushed to the street. "Where?" she asked him as she flagged down a cab.

"Connelly building, seventh floor. Armed…he's armed. Dangerous. Careful." Shipley coughed hard and she waited before answering him.

"I'm coming. Don't be dead when I get there or, so help me, I'll kick your ass back down to a private. Hear me?" His laugh brought on another coughing spell then the line went dead.

Sin whistled down the next cab that drove near her and was making it across town two minutes later. She was sitting in the back of the dirty cab when it occurred to her that her discussion with herself about Payton was taken out of her hands. This way…and she refused to think of it as the coward's way out, it was a clean break. Too bad her heart didn't agree.

~~~

Payton woke up and knew immediately something was wrong. He was alone in the bed for one thing, and the room had been neatened up. He reached for his folded pants on the chair and took out his cell phone. Three missed calls and one text. None of them from Sydney. Pulling on his pants, he went to the bathroom.

He tried dialing her twice while he pulled on his shoes and both times it went to voicemail. He was ready to toss the thing across the room when it vibrated. He had to answer his mom.

"I suppose I should be happy you were there when they carted my body away in the ambulance," his mom said in way of greeting. "I guess it's an everyday thing for you when your own mother gets kidnapped at gun point, beaten up, and used as a human shield."

He had to laugh despite the pain where his heart used to be. "I'm coming now. I had…I had something I needed to do before I could come in. Have you seen Shaller?"

"No. That nice young doctor friend of yours, Doctor Waite, was in. He said she would be in surgery for a bit longer to set her arm." There was just enough of a pause in her conversation to make him want to tell her to be quiet. "I don't suppose that young woman is related to him, is she? And will she be coming with you?"

Payton got into the car. How could he tell her he didn't know? He didn't know if he'd hurt her, broken her heart, or she had an errand to run. He was getting tired of her taking off, but this time he knew it was completely his fault. So he didn't answer about Sydney.

"I'll be there in a few minutes. And yes. Sydney is his sister. I love you, Mom."

Payton tried her cell again before he pulled out into traffic. This time it rang before ending up at her voicemail. And like before, he didn't leave a message.

He wasn't sure what to say to her, first of all. He was pissed at her, but more so at himself. He wasn't sure about a few things as well.

Had he hurt her physically and that's why she left? Probably not. He was reasonably sure if she hadn't wanted what had happened between them, she would have stopped him. He grinned. She would have hurt him too. So that theory was out.

Could she have just stepped out to get a paper and donuts? He dismissed that almost as fast as he thought it. She had showered and everything was gone except for her rings.

He had removed them soon after they'd gotten the bed straightened up. He'd closed his eyes for about a minute or two when he'd pulled her close to him and she whimpered. He'd never meant to leave them on that long and felt bad about it.

Then there was the fact that she wasn't answering his calls. Okay, he thought, there could be any number of reasons why she wasn't answering. Dead battery, for one thing. She could have forgotten to turn it back on. Hell, she might have broken it when she'd saved his mom. But that just didn't feel right.

He was at the front desk at the hospital searching for his mom's room when Alyssa walked up and handed him Connor.

"Your mom is really nice. She said you and Sin saved her life."

Payton kissed Connor before saying anything. "Sydney did all the work. I was just window dressing."

When she snorted he looked at her. "Sin doesn't strike me as a woman who would have need for window dressing to get a job done. Come on, I'll take you to your mom's room."

Alyssa was stepping into the elevator when she said something that made him pause. "Roger Shipley, do you know him?" Payton nodded. "He called Cain earlier. He was looking for Sin."

"Did Cain tell him where she was?" Payton's heart was pounding hard. He'd never thought about her going to find the shooter with Shipley.

"He didn't know, well, not for sure. We thought she was with you." She looked at him before she continued. "Anyway, he gave him her cell and told him the house number just in case. Funny thing," she said just as they got off the ride to his mom's floor.

"What?" he asked as he stayed on the ride.

"Cain said the man...Shipley, Sin calls him, Cain said he sounded winded. He thought maybe he should have been in better shape just getting out of the service and all. Sin certainly is wouldn't— Where the hell are you going?"

Payton shoved Connor into her arms and took off down the hall back toward the elevators.

"I'm going to kick Sydney's ass then marry her." Payton thought he heard Alyssa shout back "about time," but wasn't sure. He pulled out his cell and called his mom's room.

"Sydney's in trouble and I have to find her. Then I'm going to marry her whether she wants to or not."

"Well of course you are," him mom answered. "But Payton, I'm not so sure I would point out to her that you believe she's in trouble until you're sure she is. I do believe she would have no problems making you very aware of just how capable she really is."

Payton agreed. "I'm sorry, Mom. We had… She and I… We…"

"Darling, whatever it is you're trying hard not to say, I understand. You had a spat and now she needs you. I'll be waiting with your grandma's ring when the two of you get back. Alyssa has offered me the use of her very lovely home while I'm here." She lowered her voice as she continued. "Did you know that Alyssa is Nathan Howard's daughter?"

"Yes, ma'am. And so you know, I'm going to be living here from now on too. Sydney and her family are close and I want her to be happy."

They talked until he got to his car before they hung up. Then he called someone he was sure could help them. "Colonel Patterson? It's Payton Cooperider. How do I get in touch with Roger Shipley?"

~Chapter 20~

Roger looked down at his chest. Blood stained it completely. Even the tops of his pants were soaked through. He knew it was only a matter of time, minutes really, before he was dead. But he needed to wait for Sydney. He needed to talk to her, tell her what he'd found out.

"Boy, if we ain't a fucking pair," the voice deeper in the building said.

Shipley didn't bother answering him. He wasn't sure he had the strength anyway. Coughing again, he watched blood pour from chest wound.

"I'm gonna enjoy killing you, Shipley. And the fat bonus because I do it is gonna go a long way to setting me up real nice like. Plus, you should know I'm gonna kill that bitch too. General Magellan is going to come out of his retirement just to see the bitch shot in front of a firing squad for that stupid trick she played on him about the brassieres. He said once she's out of the picture he's gonna press the president into how it's not safe for women in the line of combat."

Shipley looked down at the recorder on his leg. Still running. He'd never been so happy for a door prize winnings in his life.

He'd walked into a new Dollar General, going in for some soap and some other personals, when he'd been deemed the one hundredth customer since they opened. He'd won the tiny digital recorder and a one hundred dollar gift card.

"Shipley? You still breathing?"

Barnes, Dale Barnes, had been the one who had betrayed his country, his comrades, and his commanding officer. All for a bit of money.

"Yeah, still kicking." But for how much longer? he wondered. Shipley didn't think much. He was fading out quicker now and staying under a lot longer according to the timer on the recorder. "How's your wound doing? Capt got you pretty good, huh?"

"Fucking whore. I'm gonna enjoy killing that bitch. If she hadn't shot me I'd be sitting on a plane to Belize right now. They got no taxes down that 'a way."

Shipley heard it. It was slight, barely audible, but he was close to the door. He tuned out the rest of what Barnes was saying to try and focus on staying conscious until she arrived.

Shipley wasn't sure why he knew it was Sydney, but he was. He'd called her about ten minutes ago, just after he'd been shot the second time, the one to his chest. He'd been stupid not bringing her along with him to go after Barnes. But Shipley had wanted to be her hero. To be the one to save the day. He loved her very much, loved her like the daughter he'd never had.

He knew Barnes was the one who had betrayed them. He'd found it out the third week he'd been working his way up the chain of command to get closer to Wickett. He'd been going up the sidewalk toward Wickett's house when he and Barnes had been coming out. Shipley had just enough time to duck behind another car before either man had looked his way.

After Wickett had gone to bed later that night Shipley had broken into his house and found a file on Barnes and him, plus a great deal more information about a few others. Shipley had turned everything over to Patterson except for the file on Barnes a few weeks later. He kept that one for himself. He'd made copies of them all, including the one on Detective Cooperider, anyway.

Closing his eyes, he thought about the last several hours. He'd watched the cops fumble around for twenty minutes after the shooting in the lot. Two of them had actually stepped in blood. But Shipley had seen enough sniper shots to know how to trace a shot back to the source. He found what he'd been looking for on top of some accounting place five minutes after he saw the Capt being ushered none too gentle like to a car and driven away. He didn't worry about her. She wouldn't have gone anywhere she didn't want to.

After he'd found the building where the shot had come from, he simply traced the blood back through the building and to the street. The blood wasn't much of a trail, but every time Barnes had had to stop he'd leave a bigger pool of himself behind. By the time Shipley got to the Donnelly building three blocks away he knew Barnes was in trouble.

Shipley might have killed Barnes right off except, in his arrogance, he'd assumed that Barnes would be a bit closer to death than he'd been and had gotten the jump on him. Shipley had shot at Barnes, but wasn't all that sure he'd hit him. Barnes, however, shot Shipley in the chest and arm, dropping him near the door.

When something touched his leg Shipley didn't even have the strength to raise his gun. It was just as well; he might have shot Sydney if he had. As it was all he could do was smile at her.

They had worked together for the better part of seven years. And had been on plenty of missions together where communicating verbally would get someone killed and they so didn't want to get killed. So they had developed their own type of sign language. Now he was nearly too weak to work them out, but she seemed to understand him. From the look on her face he'd say she understood a great deal more than he was telling her. She knew he was as close to death as his next breath.

"You still breathing, sarge?" The question from Barnes startled them both. "Anytime you wanna quit is fine by me."

Shipley grabbed Sydney's arm when she started to move. "I got too much life in me just yet," he said loud enough for Barnes to hear, but he looked directly at Sydney. "I got plenty more to say to you."

When she nodded he laid back, spent. He had to hang on for her. He had to tell her what he'd found. Information she needed.

~~~

Sydney moved into the shadows of the vacant building. She needed a minute so she leaned heavily back against the wall as she thought about Shipley.

He was as good as dead. And he knew it too. She wanted to demand that he let her call a squad, but knew he'd refuse. She also knew that, like her, he didn't want any heroics done to save him and, by God, she'd make sure he didn't get any.

The building was a mess. She'd seen it a few times when she'd been out and had remembered it from her childhood. She thought it had been abandoned then too. She was moving over some empty crates when she found the body.

The man had been there for at least a year, if that. Even in the darkened area he was in she could see that he'd been shot. The neat hole between where his eyes had been looked to be made by a large caliber gun. Most likely a Glock. He was dressed similar to her, dark clothes, heavy boots. He had on a light jacket so she thought he'd either been here less than she'd thought or he'd had been dead longer, as it was nearly freezing outside and he wasn't dressed for this kind of weather. She stepped around his body, giving him and any evidence that might still remain a wide berth.

Sin heard the man talking when she'd been with Shipley, but it wasn't until she saw him that she recognized him. Dale Barnes and, Christ almighty, he was bragging about having her killed. And also how he'd felt it was his duty as a United States soldier to make sure things remained a man's army.

"Can you believe they let a God damned woman lead us?" he was asking presumably Shipley. "She should have been home raising brats, but the fucking dyke was out shouting orders at us like we were her fucking servants."

Sydney heard Shipley laugh. It was a sharp bark of laughter then he was coughing again. But he hadn't answered and that scared her more than Barnes did.

As she moved into a better position to take Barnes out, she tried to remember if he'd ever given any clue that he was in with Magellan. He'd make some comments about it being a man's place. Hell, she did too. But they had laughed it off or so she'd thought. She rounded the next wall when she remembered something else, something he'd said when they'd landed just outside of the Air force base that first day.

"Well gents, and you, Captain Waite, it's been a real pleasure knowing you all. I hope you all know it's been well worth it and all in good fun."

They'd laughed at him...not with him, now that she thought about it, but at him. He was always fucking it up when he tried to say something profound or clever and they'd all thought that's what he'd been doing then. But he wasn't. He was giving them all the middle finger basically.

When she had him in front of her she looked at him, really looked at him. He was young, she realized with a start. She'd always assumed he was about Shipley's age, but he was probably closer to Payton's and hers. But he was fat where they were both lean, saggy where they were toned, and he was as bald as they came. She supposed that she'd been looking more at his abilities, or the lack thereof, as a soldier rather than as a man.

She must have made a sound because he suddenly turned to her with his weapon pointed at her. She had hers pointing at him as well. She could see then that he was bleeding. There was a stain of blood on his right shoulder and a pool of it under his leg. The blood loss was a great deal.

"Well, hello there. Have you made peace with your momma, girl?"

She thought it was an odd question so ignored it. "You fucked up, Barnes. Messing with what's mine. I'd like to take you back to a trial, but...well, I don't think you're gonna make it." She grinned at him. "Drop the gun and I'll get you some medical help. I want you to be nice and healthy when you stand before a firing squad."

"Fuck you, bitch. You're gonna die long before me." She fired when he did.

She had to crawl back to Shipley and was terrified when she got to him that he'd died. When he opened his eyes and looked at her, for several seconds she thought he didn't know who she was.

"You hurt?" She nodded and he closed his eyes again. "I'm as good as dead, captain, but don't let them do nothing that will prolong this shit."

"I won't. I promise you." She moved to the space between his legs and knew that nothing in this world, not even if they were here right now, would save him. "You should have waited for me."

She watched him breathe and when he finally spoke she had to lean forward to hear him. "You're not going to be happy with my tale, but I'm afraid—" His coughing cut him off. "I'm not going to be telling it all. One door opens and a whole set of mysteries open up for you and not a one of them helps. You're gonna have to watch your back from now on, you and that lover boy cop."

"Shipley, I never told you this before, but your timing really sucks and you tell a story like shit."

He laughed then he coughed again. "Your mother? She ain't no saint. Your daddy wasn't either, but I'm guessing you already figured that one out. She is—" This time, blood poured from his mouth when he started to cough. "Sydney, I have loved you like my own. Be happy."

Sin watched him struggle and knew that he wasn't going to say anymore. When he took a hitching breath, she cried when the blood on his chest seemed to suddenly stop flowing. In her head she knew he was gone. It was her heart that couldn't come to grips with it. She pulled out her cell phone and called the police to tell them where she was.

~Chapter 21~

Payton was trying to remain calm. *Trying* to remain calm was a lot more work than he thought it should have been. He started pacing outside the yellow tape again when he heard his name being called. He looked up at Cain as he strode toward him, speaking before he got there.

"Band-aid ripped off quickly or peeled back slowly? I'm a slow, take my time kind of guy. You know…build up to—"

"What the fuck are you talking about? How is Sydney and when can I see her?" Payton could feel the tension hike to new levels in his body when Cain frowned. "She's hurt."

"Yes," Cain said, then frowned again. "She'd been shot. Upper right shoulder. She won't let me near her yet."

When Cain looked at the warehouse, so did Payton. They watched as a group of MP's, or Military Police, was being led by David Patterson. This couldn't be good.

"They're going to arrest her, aren't they?" Payton asked no one in particular. He started forward as he spoke. "She's a civilian now, they have no right."

Cain grabbed his arm to stop him. "They seem to think they do. So does she. But that's not the issue."

Cain pointed to an area away from the crowds. And when they were perhaps a good ten yards away, he continued.

"She won't let them touch her friend until he's pronounced," Cain whispered to him. "She won't even let me touch her to see if she needs immediate care."

Pronounced? Dead? Who the hell was— "Shipley. She's making sure he's gone before she lets anyone near him." Cain nodded. "Did he have a DNR in his jacket too?"

Payton didn't say anything about Sydney and her midnight run with a suicide attempt, but he did wonder if this was what this was all about.

"Jacket? Oh you mean his file. I'm not sure. She mentioned it. I'm not...they'll shoot her if she doesn't let them near him soon. I don't...she wouldn't listen to me. She actually called me the enemy and threatened me."

Payton could almost feel sorry for Cain. He was glad that they had ignored her request when she had been hurt, but Payton didn't think he'd ever forget her anguish that night. He shuddered when he thought about what could have happened had he not followed her outside.

"Let me try and talk to her." He wasn't sure if she'd listen to him either, but he needed to try. "I can make her see reason. She'll—"

"She'll not trust you either," a familiar voice said behind him.

Payton turned around to see his mom. "What are you doing here?" He took a deep breath when she raised a brow at him. "I'm glad to see you, but shouldn't you be resting?"

"Peshaw. I'll rest when I'm old. Let me go in to speak to her. I know that she'll listen to me. She and I have something in common the rest of you don't know."

Payton had told his mom everything when he didn't have any luck with David Patterson. He'd gone to the hospital to see her and his sister after David had told him he couldn't help him, it was a military issue.

"You'll have to clear it with David. He's in charge. Mrs. Cooperider…Payton, you both should be aware, they've found two other bodies in the building with them. That isn't counting Shipley and another man." Cain looked uncomfortable as he continued. "They've both been murdered and it's been awhile."

Payton nodded then looked at his mom as she spoke. "Thank you, young man. You don't worry about your sister. I'll make sure she's fine."

David met them at the entrance. He looked pissed and Payton had to bite his lips to keep from laughing at him.

"She is the most stubborn woman—do you know she threatened to shoot my dick off. Then she had the nerve to—" David stopped pacing and looked at Payton's mom. "Beg pardon, ma'am. Captain Waite brings out the worst in me at times."

She smiled. "I would imagine she brings out the best as well. Let me go in with Payton and we'll have her out in no time."

So they were lead to the seventh floor of the building were six MP's were standing around with their weapons drawn and pointed at the back of the room. It wasn't until David had them move back that he could see Sydney.

She looked like hell. She had been running her fingers thorough her hair again, he could see. It was a habit he'd noticed she had when she was deep in thought. It stood up on end and curled everywhere. Her face was pale, her lips looked like they were swollen, and there was no color in them either. She was covered in blood; her arm hung lank at her side. But it was how she was sitting that disturbed him.

Shipley was leaning against the wall; his eyes were closed. Blood covered his chin and his shirt was red it was so saturated. Even from the doorway where he stood Payton could see he was no longer breathing. But the closer he got, the more his heart broke.

Sydney was holding her gun in her left hand. She wasn't pointing it at anyone, but she did have her finger on the trigger. She was sitting between Shipley's outstretched legs, but not touching him. She was protecting her man and friend even after death.

His mom moved forward. Payton wanted to tell her to be careful. He'd even opened his mouth to do so, but she sent him a look back that had him snap his mouth closed.

"Stop where you are," Sydney said to her. "I don't have any idea who you are, but I will shoot your fucking head off. I'm waiting for the military to get off their fucking asses and tell me my man is gone. Until then, I'm not fucking moving."

"It's nice to know our government moves like our police force does," his mom said as she sat down on one of the crates near them. "You know they waited a full hour when my husband was killed before they remembered someone should have called it? I'm sure it wasn't something that happens every day, but—"

"I wouldn't count on it. Every time you think the rules are in stone, some fuck-tard goes and changes them. When I said no heroics, I fucking meant no heroics," Sydney snapped as she lifted the gun. "You're a civilian. You should get out of here."

Payton watched the MP's move as one toward the two women. But backed off immediately when David snarled at them to stand down. Candace Cooperider didn't bat an eye.

~~~

"A long time ago I married Payton's dad. He was a lovely man. I believe he would have liked you, Sydney. And you do know me, by the way. You saved my life yesterday morning." Candace looked at the young woman and saw all sorts of emotions flitter over her face. "In the mall from that dreadful man who hurt my son."

"He's dead." Sydney lowered her gun and Candace let out a slow, long breath.

"Yes, he is. Thank you for that. The man behind you, is he your friend?"

"Yes," Sydney said as she glanced at him then back at Candace. "Yes, he was one of my men when I was in the service. He said that he wanted to go out with his boots on. I can't let them take him until I'm sure."

Candace nodded. "Did Payton tell you he was adopted? So is his sister Shaller. You'll love her too, by the way. She can't wait to meet you." Candace moved off the box and onto the floor and was happy when Sydney didn't lift her gun again. "He was about three. They didn't know when exactly he was born, so they guessed. His mother wasn't sure. Anyway, we adopted him and brought him to our home."

"I guess he told you I was damaged," Sydney said softly. "Did he tell you I tried to eat a bullet too? I can't figure out why he'd care."

"Don't be stupid, girl," Candace snapped. "He loves you, that's why." Candace didn't need to turn around to know Cain had walked in and that he hadn't been aware of her attempt on her own life. But she didn't have time to deal with that right now. "And that moron that said that you were damaged is being dealt with."

"I can't...I never knew I wanted rug rats until they told me I couldn't have them." Sydney brushed at the tears falling down her cheeks. "It's probably just as well. I'd probably fuck them up mentally anyway."

"Probably," Candace agreed with a small laugh. "Of course, you might not either. You strike me as a fairly intelligent woman. Do you now or have you ever eaten worms or tried to dress a dog in a dress?" Candace laughed at the expression on Sydney's face before she finished. "Payton ate worms as a child and poor Bagley, our dog, would run for cover whenever Shaller came into the room. The dog had a horrible fear of dresses for years after that."

Sydney looked down at the gun in her hand as she spoke. Candace held her breath and hoped this was going to be the breaking point. And in a good way.

"Shipley said...he said that he loved me. Said I was the daughter he'd never had. I couldn't let them take him without being sure. Without being sure he was gone." She looked up at Candace. "He begged me not to let them make him into some pin cushion all in the name of medical science."

Candace felt her heart go out to the young woman. She was hurting so badly for what she was doing and not one of the men in the room with them could see it. She moved closer to her and put out her hand.

"I know you couldn't, dear. I need you to be sure too. I need that as well, I believe. When I was younger, I was a coroner of the state of Virginia. If you hand me your weapon, I'll check for you and me both."

Candace wasn't sure she would do it. Sydney was hurt, not just physically, but mentally too. But she was sure that for as much as the girl hurt, Payton would care for her and love her.

"There's something that you have to make sure only David gets. Something Shipley gave me." Sydney held out a small, blood-covered box in her hand as she whispered. "They're going to arrest me. I know that. So you have to promise you get this to David."

Candace reached out, took the box and slipped it into her pocket. "Are you going to give me your gun, dear?"

Sydney looked at her, tears and grief on her face. "I can't let it go. I want to, I really do, but it's like it's frozen in my hand."

Candace nodded and turned to Payton and motioned for him to move forward. "Let Payton take it then. And I'll confirm your man is down. All right, honey?"

Sydney nodded and Payton moved to Sydney's other side. Candace put two fingers to Shipley's throat and nodded at Sydney as Payton reached for her gun.

"He's gone. Time of death is zero three twenty-three."

"When the gun is free, you two will need to step back from Captain Waite, please," David said as he approached them. "These men are going to take her in for—"

"They hurt her and hell will be paid," Candace told him as she stepped in front of Sydney and Payton. "I'm not without my own ways of making your life a living hell."

"I assure you both that if they so much as make her whimper I will personally have them shot." David turned, but Candace grabbed his shoulder.

"She said you would need this," Candace whispered near his ear. "You had better be trustworthy or, so help me, *I'll* shoot your fucking dick off."

As soon as Payton stepped back, the MP's moved toward Sydney. Two of them helped her stand and two more began checking Shipley's body.

The men were gentle with her. One of the men spoke softly to her while the other held her steady. Candace reached for her hand and gave it a hard squeeze.

"I'm going to love having you as a daughter, Sydney."

She nodded as they cuffed her.

Payton wrapped his arm around her waist as they watched Sydney being escorted by and then he kissed her cheek. "I love you, Mom."

"She's a hell of a girl, Payton. I like her." She looked at her son. "You make sure you tell her you love her every day, young man, or I will kick your bottom."

He kissed her again. "I love you so much. But you're scary."

They walked out together and watched as they put Sydney in an ambulance. She was nodding, but they couldn't hear what was being said to her.

~Chapter 22~

Sydney looked at the table of men in front of her. She wasn't sure how to answer the question General Worth had asked her. How the hell was she supposed to know what motivated Barnes to want to kill her? She'd told them money, but that didn't seem to set well with them. Before she could ask him what the fuck he wanted her to say David touched her arm, the one not in the sling.

"I believe that question was answered yesterday and, if memory serves, the day before that as well. Private Barnes was the only one who truly knew the answer to that and, thanks to Captain Waite, he's no longer a threat to our national security." David stood up as he continued. "You've listened to the recordings a total of nine times over the past four days. If you don't have what you need by now, then I'm not sure what to tell you."

"And where do you think you're going, Captain Waite? These hearings are for—"

The general was cut off by a commotion at the rear of the room. Sydney snapped to attention, as did every other man in the room. When the President of the United States walked in no one sat or slumped over.

"Gentlemen," he began before turning to her. "Hello, Captain Waite. How's your shoulder? I heard you'd been injured a few days ago."

"Yes sir, it's fine, sir. But it's not captain anymore. I keep trying to tell these yahoos...men, but they won't listen to me." She glanced at David when he made a slight noise. "Lieutenant Colonel Patterson said he called someone on my behalf. I didn't know it was you, sir. He should have kept his mouth shut."

The President glanced at David before turning back to her. "He didn't call me. Your sister-in-law did. Alyssa has a way with words, doesn't she?"

Sydney flushed. "I don't know her all that well, sir. I've been...I've had other things on my agenda lately."

She had been in the brig or military jail since she'd been escorted from the building eight days ago. She'd been escorted to and from this building in Washington D.C. for the past five days and had only seen one other person besides those in this room once, and that was the surgeon. She'd been cooperative up until now, but she wanted to go home.

"So you have. And you are still a captain until I say otherwise. Have a seat," he told her when he pulled out her chair. "Let me see if I can get this thing finished once and for all. Oh, when this is over I'd like to discuss a job opportunity with you."

"Sir, my friend...Sergeant Shipley's funeral is today. I would like...I need to be there. He was one of my men, sir. I want to be there when he is put to rest."

He patted her on the shoulder. "As he was one of mine, captain. You'll be there. I'll make sure."

They'd given her her captain's uniform to wear to these proceedings so she was dressed in her formal dress blues, as were the men behind the table. And since she'd had it drilled into her head that respect meant standing at attention until told to do otherwise, she did just that. She supposed it didn't matter to her how she was dressed. So long as the President of the United States was standing, so was she.

She glanced at David again and watched him nod to the other men who'd come in with the President. Secret Service men, she thought, and dismissed them as background noise. It was the lovely woman who'd come in with them that had her attention. Sydney listened as she addressed the men at the table.

"These are signed affidavits stating that Captain Waite was acting with the full backing of the President and for the interest of the United States Government when she and Sergeant Shipley infiltrated the ring that eventually led to the arrest of soon to be discharged men who acted against our government…your government. The trial pending on the trial of nine members of the United States Military versus the United States Government will commence as soon as next month. Here are other affidavits stating that Captain Waite and Sergeant Shipley acted with the full authority of the President. These affidavits state that—"

"Are you goin' to keep giving us this paperwork until you flood our desks with—"

"General Murphy, correct?" At his nod the woman continued. "General Murphy, I will flood your house with paperwork if I feel the need. You'll need to shut up and let me do my job or I'll have these nice gentlemen in the black suits put you in the cell Captain Waite has been keeping warm for you."

"Perhaps," the President said with ill-masked humor, "this will go much better if we get to the point. Captain Waite did her job. The one *I* asked her to do. Does anyone have any questions?"

No one said a word. The President nodded then walked to the table and shook the hand of each man still standing. Before Sydney could gather her wits she was being escorted out again, this time by the Secret Service, David, and the President to the waiting car. They were driving away when she spoke up.

"What job?" Both men, David and the President, looked at her oddly. "What job did you tell me to do?"

"Protect and serve. You've never been officially discharged. I kept getting the incorrect papers across my desk." The President looked at David who flushed pink. "Then this came across my desk about a month ago."

He handed her a thick file. She opened it then closed it quickly. It was a picture of her when she'd been shot in the jungle.

"It was hard for me to look at it as well." He nodded to David who continued.

"The bullets that were taken from your body matched the ones used in a shooting last year when an attempt was made on your sister Quinn's life." Sydney looked up sharply from the closed file in her lap. "Then three days ago we found several more in the body of the two dead men in that warehouse with you."

"You don't think I had anything—"she snapped at him.

"Christ, no. No, we don't. We never did. But there's more…the bullet retrieved from Detective Cooperider was a match as well. Someone connects them all, to you, your family, and to Cooperider." He looked at the President. "Someone wants you all dead."

"The man…the one that shot me, he said that he was getting a bonus for killing me. He said he'd been hired to kill us all, but was getting more for my death." She thought of something Shipley had said as well. "Shipley told me that I needed to watch my back. That every door opened another mystery. I don't know what he meant. Then he told me Guinevere isn't a saint."

David was nodding. "We read the transcript of the tape. He mentioned your father too. Do you know what that was about?" David knew she hadn't seen much of her family since she'd enlisted. It hadn't been until after her father's death that she'd even considered coming home again for a visit.

"No. My father was glad to see the back of me and me of well of him. He was a bastard of the highest order and couldn't have improved much with age." Sydney looked out the window. "He'd tried to kill Quinn over some money a few years ago."

The limo slid to a smooth stop and it was several seconds before they were lead from the limo to a tarmac where Air Force One sat. She stopped so suddenly that the Secret Service behind her bumped into her.

"I can't get on that." Everyone looked at the plane then at her. "That's for the President. I'm a…I'm a…"

"Going to be late if you don't get a move on," the President said as he pulled her along. "And since I'm the President, I'm saying it's okay if you ride with me."

It wasn't until she was inside the plane that she got her tongue back. "Late for what? Where are you...am I being shot?"

She had no idea why that thought popped in her head, but if they were going to do it she wanted to say goodbye to a couple of people. At least her family, then she thought she'd beg to get one to Payton too.

"No. Buckle." She did as David told her. "The things that spill out of your mouth amaze me. We're going to Shipley's funeral. The President is going to say a few words and you are going to be a good girl and do what you're told. Right?"

"You know I've never been one to follow rules blindly," she muttered softly.

David's laugh was full and loud. "There's an understatement if I've ever heard one. You don't even follow them when it's all laid out in neat order for you."

"So? I like things understood from the get-go. How many times have my questions kept us from being FUBAR, huh?" She stood up to yell at him more. "You said yourself that—"

Suddenly, she was grabbed from behind and turned. She had a fleeting thought that the men in suits were after her then she smelled Payton. His mouth was so close that she could feel his warmed breath.

"Christ, woman. Don't you ever *not* argue with someone?" Then he was kissing her.

~~~

Payton pulled her closer as she leaned into him. Nothing in this world felt better than her body next to his. When he heard someone clear their throat again he pulled back but couldn't let her go.

The President, the man who had arranged for him to be here, was smiling. "You two will need to take a seat. We will be ready to go soon."

With another quick kiss, he led her to the couch. The seatbelts were strapped around them and, suddenly, they were moving.

"How are you? God, I've missed you," he told her softly. "David's been giving us updates when he could. He said you'd been before a bunch of asses that didn't know what they were talking about."

"That pretty much sums it up. I'm fine. Your mom...she's okay then? And your sister?" Then she glanced away. "Why are you here, Payton? I mean, I thought...didn't we say that we needed to..." She took a deep breath and started again. "I thought you were going to move on."

He moved a lock of hair from her eye and smiled. "No. I'm just where I want to be from now on." He was suddenly nervous. His mom had told him to get her to say yes before she talked herself and him out of getting married. He thought she might be right. After they had the okay to unbuckle and move about the plane he did so, then he reached into his pocket and pulled out the ring.

It had been his grandma's ring then his mom's when she'd first married his dad. His sister hadn't wanted to use it when she'd married. It wasn't until recently that they found out it wasn't that she didn't want to use it, but her husband didn't. He thought it was too common.

The yellow diamond was anything but common. It was very rare, as a matter of fact. It was two carats of pure beauty as far as he was concerned. It glimmered now against the roof of the cabin they were in and off every part of the room. The diamond itself was surrounded in white and blue diamonds all about a quarter carat each. The yellow gold band was inlaid with white gold hearts. He pulled her hand into his and held it to the tip of her finger. He slipped to the floor effortlessly.

"Marry me. I love you with all my heart. Marry me, please?" When she didn't answer right way he slipped the ring all the way to her knuckle and waited. He thought she would explode quicker if he did it and wasn't surprised when she did.

"I can't marry...are you nuts? Of course you are." She started to pull it off, but he grabbed her hand again. "I can't marry you, Payton. You have to know that."

"I know no such thing. You're already sleeping with me, why not marry me?" He grinned when she flushed and looked around. "My mom said you had to make an honest man out of me. She said you owe her and she'd hate to have to kick your butt for me." His mom had actually said much more than that, but he wasn't sharing that with the strangers in the room. Especially one of them being the President.

Payton smiled when Sydney snorted. "You're full of shit. Why?"

He looked at her while he waited for her to elaborate. When she didn't he went with his heart to try and answer what he thought she needed to hear. "Because I love you. It's as simple as that, Sydney. Isn't that enough?"

She looked at him then leaned her forehead to his. "But what about the other thing," she whispered. "You know, kids?"

"We'll have plenty. I've been talking to some new friends of ours." He pointed toward the President. "He said we'll have no problems adopting all we can handle."

"What if—" She was cut off by the pilot telling them they were ready to land, they needed to buckle back in.

It hadn't taken long to fly from Washington to Ohio where Shipley was being buried. Payton wondered if Sydney knew that and wasn't surprised when she'd asked him.

"Why aren't we taking him home? I mean, he had a house in Louisiana. I thought he'd be buried there."

David answered before Payton could. "He'd made arrangements to be buried here several months ago. He'd even bought a house here after selling the one down south."

She didn't say anything as they got off the plane and into another limo. But he could tell she was thinking hard. She would be worried about his family, the one that David had told him that had wanted nothing to do with the man who had chosen the Army life over them. They had hung up on David, he'd told Payton.

They were headed straight to the gravesite. Shipley hadn't wanted a regular service, but simply a graveside service. Payton didn't think the city of Zanesville was too happy about the arrangements, but had worked hard to grant the wishes of a fallen hero.

Payton looked at the lines of cars they drove by as they headed to the site. There must have been five hundred vehicles lined on both sides of the road leading up to the small cemetery.

It seemed that every soldier, active or retired, had shown up to honor one of their own. Payton looked over at Sydney dressed in her parade uniform and then down at his own. He too was here to honor a man he'd come to like over the past few days.

Payton walked to the hearse with David and the President. He was startled to see the latter man get in line to be a pall bearer.

David leaned close and whispered to him. "Stay with Sydney, son. This is going to be hard on her. We'll take him home." Payton nodded and walked back to Sydney.

~Chapter 23~

Sydney looked around at all of the people who had come to the grave. She bit back a smile knowing that Shipley would have been royally pissed about all this. She looked over at Payton when he squeezed her hand.

"He would have hated this," he whispered in her ear.

"I was thinking the same thing. It was what I wanted too. No press, no people, especially no military."

She looked over as the casket was being brought to the grave. Six men held him up and three men with rifles walked on either side of them with one leading the way. David was on Shipley's left and the President on his right. The flag lifted slightly in the breeze, but settled down again over the oak repository.

Sydney hadn't been to many military funerals even though she'd spent the last ten years in the service in the front line. When a man died in the line of duty she would take a set of his dog tags and make sure the other set was out where it was visible for the next group to come through to pick them up. She knew that they would make note of the name and outfit he or she had been with before taking the body back to whatever ship was going home. She knew the name of every man she'd taken a tag off of.

When Shipley was at rest everyone who could sat down. Sydney sat down with her family, Payton, David, and then Candace. The woman had hugged Sydney so tight earlier that she thought there might be a mark later. It had felt wonderful.

The eulogy was given by the President. He talked about Shipley's years of service, his death for his country, and the honor that he'd felt having had a man like Roger Shipley work and serve for him.

David talked about the man. "When I first met Shipley he was in a bar room brawl. There were several men already laid out on the floor bleeding from various places, but none of them moved. Shipley had his beefy arm around this little private and saying any number of things he was going to do to when he let go."

Sydney smiled, remembering.

"Now at first glance, you'd say this man is a nuisance and needs to be put in irons and then thrown in the brig. But he hadn't done anything other than hold onto the private until help could arrive. He told me while he, himself, hadn't thrown a single punch, it was the private in his arm had done the ass kicking. But he did feel it necessary to say that it was justified all around."

Several men she had served with turned to her and she smiled and shrugged at them. She heard Payton laugh and Cain groan.

"Two months later," David continued. "Sergeant Shipley asked to have the private put on his squad. He and

Captain Waite, the private back then, had been together since."

"What happened in the bar?" the President asked then flushed when everyone turned to him. "I'm sorry. I would like to know what they did to her to have her lay them all out."

David turned to her. "Captain Waite?"

She flushed again as she stood. Several of her men were laughing now. She stood up. "I was shooting pool and winning. They accused me of cheating."

"But you were cheating, Capt. You was good at it, but you was cheating," someone shouted over the laughter.

"Yes, I was, but he said I was cheating by wiggling my as...butt, not cheating on the table. He said I was distracting him and the others from watching the plays." She looked at David before she finally told him the truth. "All I did was plunk him on the head when he smacked my bottom. Shipley was holding me so I wouldn't go after the other man who said my tits were distracting as well. He wanted a...he wanted to cop a feel of them. I took exception to that."

Everyone that hadn't been laughing before was doing so now, including the President. David nodded to her and ended his talk when she sat down. Payton leaned over to her and nipped hard on her neck before he spoke softly to her.

"No one touches your ass again but me. Understood?"

She nodded, not trusting her voice.

"And when I get you home I'm going to show you who should be spanking that ass."

Sydney didn't move. She could feel her body respond to his promise by her nipples hardening and her pussy creaming. She looked down at the ring he'd put on her finger.

It occurred to her that she hadn't answered him. Not that she knew what she would say when he pressed. She did love him with all her heart, but marry him? She wasn't sure. It wasn't until they fired the twenty-one gun salute and one of the men handed her Shipley's flag that she knew her answer.

~~~

Payton watched her closely. Something had changed since they'd left the cemetery and come to Cain and Alyssa's home. He wasn't sure if it was a good change or not, but he did intend to find out what it was. Before he could get to her to ask he was waylaid by Captain Grant.

"Detective Cooperider? I was wondering if I may have a word or two with you, please? I understand you have a grudge against Richard Conway? Is that true?"

"I don't know a Richard...the man who was engaged to Sydney? Yeah, I do. But I haven't talked to the man." *Yet*, he added mentally, but he would, and soon. "Why, has he said something?"

"No, not to me at any rate. You say that he was engaged to Sydney?" She glanced back at the woman in question who was currently shaking hands with the President's wife. "He's the one who told her she wasn't good enough for him?"

Payton nodded, but said nothing. He didn't know how she'd come by that information, but had a good idea. His mother, he would guess.

"I was wondering if I could persuade you to come down to the office tomorrow sometime. I'd like a word with you."

Payton had plans for tomorrow and for the rest of tonight as soon as he could get Sydney alone. "No, here is fine. What can I help you with, captain?"

She laughed; it was a knowing laugh. "All right. I would like you to consider staying here and becoming a part of my force. I sort of had a long conversation with your chief in Jersey and he had a lot to say about you."

Payton looked over at his chief and when he winked back, Payton cringed. "I'm sure you shouldn't believe half of what he's told you and none of the rest. He's pissed off because I quit today."

Cait laughed again. "He said I'd be damn lucky if you didn't have my job in a few years. Said you were one of his best officers and if you didn't take the job he was going to kick your ass."

Payton thought there was an awful lot of that going around lately. It seemed everyone wanted a piece of his ass. He glanced back over at Sydney. She was the only one he was actually looking forward to taking a bite out of it.

"She going to marry you?" Cait asked.

Payton looked at the police captain then back at Sydney. "She hasn't answered me yet. She's sort of hung up on what Conway told her being gospel. I could care less if we only had each other for the next fifty years."

Cait nodded then waved Cain and Alyssa over. "Doctor Waite, I was wondering if you found a family to take that little girl that was abandoned at the hospital last week?"

"No. No one wants her. If I can't find someone soon she'll be put in the system. I'd hate that. Alyssa and I were thinking we'd take her ourselves if no one else comes around." He winked at Payton. "Connor could use a little sister, or even a cousin, don't you think?"

Payton looked between the three of them and then threw back his head and laughed. "Slick move, guys. So when do we get to take her home?"

Cain laughed too and then nodded in Sydney's direction. "You can have her as soon as Sin says yes."

They got home around midnight. When Sydney walked to the kitchen Payton followed her. She had pulled down two glasses and got out the jug of tea he'd made for her that morning. He sat down at the table and waited. He knew she had something to tell him. He wasn't sure what had transpired between her and the President, but he was willing to bet it was a job.

"Cain is having someone make a frame for the flag." She sat down and started playing with one of the five stars that were in the triangle. "He said that Shipley's name and birth date would be inscribed on it."

"That'll be nice. We'll put it someplace special." He waited. "The lawyer, he wants you to come and see him Wednesday, right? We'll make a day of it in Columbus if you want."

Still nothing important. "His family said they didn't want it. They said they didn't want anything to do with him. They told me to keep the flag."

"Sydney, honey, what is it?" She had tears in her eyes when she looked back at him. "Ah, baby, don't cry."

He walked over and scooped her up into his arms. Then he sat down with her in his lap. He held her while she sobbed. He knew she was hurt, hurt because of his family, the loss of her friend, and everything else that had been going on since he'd met her. He held her until she stopped and stirred.

When she stood up and sat back down on his lap facing him, he groaned. "If you want to play then why don't we go up to the bedroom?"

"Here is fine. I want to take you this time. I want you to feel like you make me feel. Will you let me?"

He could hear the soft tone of need in her voice, but it was the hard bite of wanting him that had him saying yes. When she stood again he waited for her to make the first move. When she did he nearly swallowed his tongue.

"I want to ride you. But don't touch me. If you do then I'm going to splinter into a thousand pieces and I don't want that yet." She took off her blouse with all the medals pinned to it and tossed it over the chair next to them. "Then I want you to take me hard on the table. Make me come hard and quick. Undo your pants, Payton, just your pants."

He nearly stood, but didn't. He watched her while she took off her dress pants and tossed them along with her panties to the other chair that held her blouse. He was still sitting there with his hand on his belt when she was naked and delicious-looking.

"Give me your nipple. I want to suckle it." She shook her head at his demand. When she lifted her breasts up and thumbed her nipples he nearly leapt out of the chair to get her.

"Pants, Payton. I'm getting very bored waiting for you. I might have to take matters into my own hands and do this myself."

He wanted her to. He wanted to see her take herself to new heights. When her hands skimmed down her breasts and to her waist he moaned as he rubbed his hand over his covered cock. When she leaned back against the edge of the table he moved his hand to his belt and opened it. While he watched and freed his cock she lifted one leg and rested it on his thigh while she teased herself with her finger.

"Touch yourself. Open you pussy for me so I can see you pleasure yourself." His cock twitched hard in his hand as he watched her do as he'd asked. "Slide your finger into you pussy and let me taste the cream there."

Her moan went straight to his cock and wrapped around it like her hand. He fisted his cock and watched her enjoy herself. She was enjoying herself and so was he. When she leaned forward with her wet fingers, he ran his tongue along the length then suckled the digit into his mouth.

"Delicious. So spicy and hot, you even taste wet." When she stood up he nearly did as well, but she kept him there with a hand to his shoulder.

"I want to ride you, remember?" He leaned back when she moved toward him. "I want you to hold onto the seat and not touch me."

Payton nodded. He was too close to the edge to screw that up now. When she put her hand on his shoulder he steadied her with one hand at her waist. The other held his cock as she moved her wet heat over him. She looked him in the eye as she lowered herself slowly over him. When she was seated to the hilt neither of them moved, but her body, the tightening of her sheath held him, rippling around him until he thought he'd come just like this.

Her movements were slow at first. Measured and tight, she canted over him as if she really were riding him. He wanted to urge her on, to make her pick up the pace, but he didn't. He simply watched her face as she took as much pleasure as she could from him.

Payton felt her grab at him, her tight hold on him suddenly nearly strangling his cock. He wanted to surge up into her, to hold her hips steady as he pulled her down with each upward stroke. When she stiffened Payton nearly cried out with her, his own completion so close he wanted to spill himself into her. But she wanted him to take her on the table and he wanted to please her. Standing up with his hands at her ass, he moved her to the table and laid her down, her back on the table. She wrapped her legs around his waist and looked up at him, a dreamy, hungry expression on her face.

"How do you want me, baby? Hard? Fast?" He looked at her. "Both?"

"I thought of you just now. You dressed as you are taking me from behind against your cruiser. You didn't take off my clothes, just ripped off my underwear and fucked me." She surged up against him. "I'm going to come thinking about you doing that."

Christ, he nearly came too. He pulled her legs from his body and lifted her up. She looked confused for a second until he turned her around and leaned her over the table. This was going to be both.

She was wet, dripping wet and hot. He rocked into her and held her still with his hand in her hair. If either of them moved, he'd be a goner.

"Do you have any idea how badly I'd like to fuck you like that? Pull you over, get you out of the car. I wouldn't speak to you, just slam this luscious body against the hood of your car and fuck you. Hard." He felt her tighten again, her pussy ripple around him. "I don't care if you come or not. I'm in charge and when I want, I take."

Her hiss of "yes" had him rock again; her body under his moved the table. Leaning down, he nipped at her neck. She moaned.

"Do you want to come? Do you want to scream out my name, grip my cock until I come deep inside of you?" She nodded. "Marry me. Say you'll be mine forever and I'll fuck you till you can't walk."

Her legs widened slightly and she nodded again. "Please. Please make me come."

His heart was pounding. She was his. But he needed to hear it, needed her to say it to him.

"I said say it." He pulled out of her, his cock just at her entrance. "You want me to fuck you, then say it."

Sobbing, her voice loud in the room, she answered him. "Yes, I'm yours. I'll marry you, just please fuck me."

He slammed into her and heard her whimper. Standing up again, he grabbed her hips and held her to him while he moved in and out of her, slow and steady. He felt sweat drip down his back. He was going to make it last if it killed him, which he was pretty sure it would. Then he looked down. Saw his cock as it glistened with her cream, watched as he moved in and out of her and the way her ass bounced each time he entered. His climax grabbed him hard, moved through his body with lightning speed, and had him coming so hard he felt it from the top of his head to the bottoms of his feet. He heard her shouting, sobbing out his name. When he emptied himself, poured his seed into her, he collapsed, his body falling on top of hers.

Her giggle brought him around. He must have dozed for only a second or two. He lifted his head and looked down at her smiling face. "Do you usually laugh at men who take you in your kitchen?" He stood up off her and felt his cock twitch. Even after that, he still wanted her.

"I don't know. I've never been taken on any table before." She moved slowly as she stood too and turned, only to lean against the table again. "You fell asleep. You snore."

He pulled her to him and kissed her. "I do not. I love you, Sydney. Are you really going to marry me?"

Suddenly unsure, he looked at her. "Yes, I'll marry you. Take me to bed. I'm exhausted."

They gathered up her uniform and put away the mess they'd made. She went up first and he locked up. He looked at his cell phone when it vibrated in his pocket. It was Cain.

He answered with a smile. "She said yes. When can I get our daughter?"

~Chapter 24~

Sydney moved her arm under the pillow and touched her gun. She felt it there and rolled over to get the sun out of her face. She knew where she was, just didn't know why the sun was so bright. She opened one eye and looked at the window to find the curtain wide open. Snow drifted down the glass and she smiled. She looked around the rest of the room without moving.

It was a nice room. She'd never been in it before Payton was. The walls were a dark pattern of some burgundy color. She wasn't sure because the sun made it difficult to see for sure. Sydney had always preferred warm colors over the dull or bright. She supposed it had to do with having to wear drab uniforms all the time.

His furniture was big...well, she supposed it was normal-sized, but compared to her duffle it was huge. The highboy, she thought it was called, held a television, she knew. She'd seen it open when she'd come up here with him before. The carpet was a creamy color. She thought it was almost beige, but didn't care enough to ponder it. She was just moving her eyes to the other dresser when she heard a mewing sound. Rolling to her back she saw Payton looking at her. Then she saw the source of the noise.

She leapt from the bed so quickly she nearly fell. "What the fu…heck it that?"

Payton looked down at the pink bundle beside him before answering. "It's a baby. Come back to bed."

"I know it's a baby, you as…idiot. What's it doing here?" She looked around, found one of his t-shirts on the chair, and pulled it over her head. "Are you dressed? You need to get something on." She didn't know why it bothered her to be naked in front of the kid, but it did. And he was in bed…well, that didn't bother her too much. He was covered up.

"I'm dressed. I've been up since six." He lifted the blanket off him to show her he had on jeans but no shirt. "And to answer your question, she's here sleeping. Well, she was until someone took it into her head to squeal."

"I did not squeal." She sat on the bed and looked at the baby. She was looking at Sydney just like she felt. Terrified. "Whose is she?" Sydney wanted to touch her. See if her skin looked as soft as it appeared. But the thing looked ready to scream its head off so she just looked. Sydney wondered how it could move in the blanket. It was wrapped up tighter than her pack was. She looked at Payton when she realized he hadn't answered her.

"Nobody's. She was abandoned at the emergency room last week. Your brother has been caring for her until today. She had to be released."

"And she's here because…" She couldn't stand it. She reached over and started to unwrap her, making sure her fingers moved over her soft skin at least twice before getting her open. She was wrong about her skin; it was much softer than it looked.

She had on a skull cap that was a pink that defied description. Her clothes, she thought she'd heard Alyssa call it a sleeper when she'd watched Connor, was also pink. Pink with some kind of animal running up the leg. There was a clip on her jammies that had a short ribbon and a pacifier on it. The kid was sucking it like it was her last meal.

"She has to be somebody's. I know enough about biology to know that." When he didn't answer she looked at him again and it clicked. "Oh no you don't. I'm not taking this thing. You take her right back to where you got her. Tell my brother it won't work."

He sat up and started to unsnap the kid's jammies. "She's not going to be adopted. No one will take her until she's at a point where they can tell what kind of care she'll need, if any." He got her feet out of the legs of the pink and Sydney could see the tiniest little feet she'd ever seen and toes to match.

"Why would she need care? I mean, other than the normal kind kids need. She looks okay to me." Actually, Sydney thought she might be perfect. But she didn't comment.

When he pulled the jammies off her arms she lay there in a t-shirt that snapped between her legs. Sydney thought it might be nice to have one of those as an adult. Never having to tuck in your undershirt again would be heaven.

"She's a coke baby. When she came to the ER she was as high as any junkie. Her mother must have done drugs while she was pregnant and the baby got it too."

Sydney looked at him to see if he was kidding. She knew he wasn't. "Why?" She didn't know what she was asking about, but it seemed important to try to understand. The little kid didn't stop staring at her, but she did look less terrified.

"Who knows about some people? But her problems could be she'll have developmental issues, maybe learning ones as well."

He lifted the baby up and snuggled her under his chin. Sydney was mesmerized by it and was taken completely by surprise when she had the baby in her arms suddenly. She wanted to hand her back to him or at the very least put her back on the bed, but couldn't seem to do either.

"You suck, you know that?" she said to Payton without heat. "If you think I don't know what you're doing, you're full of crap."

He watched her as she held her. Sydney didn't have a clue what she was doing with the baby, but she wasn't screaming so she figured she wasn't hurting her. Payton had told her when she watched Connor that babies would let you know when you were not doing something right.

"Cait offered me a job. She wants me to be a detective on her police force." He sat up and leaned against the headboard of the bed, several pillows behind him. Sydney moved around, sat between his legs, and leaned back against him still holding the baby.

"Are you going to take it?" The kid was closing her eyes, blinking longer and longer as she was held. Sydney thought she could join her, but knew that she wouldn't be able to close her eyes so long as she held her.

"I don't know. I told her I needed to talk to you. She said she'd want me on days with her. She wants to groom me. She seems to think I'll take her job when she retires."

He wrapped his arms around her and showed her how to relax the baby against her body. He didn't let either of them go when the kid closed her eyes completely.

"The President offered me a job too. I guess technically I still work for him, but this one would be here. He wants me to train his Secret Service when he needs them and to run them through combat training when he doesn't. The place will be open to the public so no one will know what it's really for, but I'll only work with his men." She leaned her head on his shoulder. "I told him I had to talk to you first."

He kissed her cheek and didn't say anything for a little while. She was nearly dozing off when he finally spoke.

"About the baby? We need to decide. The jobs are easy compared to raising a child. I've never done it, but I've seen it. What do you want to do?"

~~~

Payton didn't say anything after he asked. He knew it was a lot to throw at her. He was actually surprised she'd been so calm so far. He had expected...he grinned. He never knew what to expect with Sydney.

"I know squat about kids, less about girls and what they need. I'm reasonably sure I was one at one time, but I've never had much to do with kids. What's her name anyway?"

Payton nuzzled Sydney's neck before answering. "Her last name will be Cooperider, the other will be left up to us, I guess. What do you think?"

"Payton, I'm serious...I don't know what to do about being her mom. My own is a piece of work. She could barely pull herself away...he said to watch her." Payton looked at her. "Shipley, he said to watch mom. And then Barnes. He said something...I don't know something like had I made amends with my mom. Why?"

She laid the baby on the bed and began to pace. Something was there, he knew it, and he was sure she'd get it. He'd read the transcript too.

"He asked you if you'd made amends with your mom then he laughed. Did he know her?"

"I don't know. Something isn't right." She started pacing again.

Neither of them figured it out and the little girl Cooperider still had no name by Wednesday. Payton had even gone to the book store and purchased a book of names. It didn't do either of them any good. For two days they called her every name they could think of and nothing stuck.

"You know," Sydney started as they drove to the attorney's office. "If we can't pick out a name for her, what the hell are we doing raising her? We're so going to suck at this."

"Oh I don't know. We had fun last night with her." They had too. They'd bought her a baby bed and spent hours putting it together. Of course it went much better after Sydney took over, but she had the instructions. He was going on male power.

The office was posh and overdone. Not two words he'd normally put together, but that's what he got. He was looking at the ugly carpet with the beautiful couch sitting on it when the secretary told them they could come in. The office wasn't any better.

The desk was tiny. Probably made smaller-looking because the man behind it was so huge. He was tall, but he might have been twice his height in girth. The man had to weigh four hundred pounds. The chairs he waved them into groaned when they sat and he sat the car seat that the baby was in as far away as he dared just in case the one he was sitting in broke.

"You have a baby. That's wonderful. What's her name?"

Payton looked at Sydney and laughed. "We're working out the details on that as we speak." The attorney, Sean Cass, looked at him oddly, but didn't comment. They had to come up with something, he thought, but said nothing.

"Mr. Shipley…err I suppose he was Sergeant Shipley, had a will made out several months ago. He came to my office and had everything all laid out in perfect order. Never seen such a big man with so much—"

Payton cut the man off. "We were told we were here because there were some legal issues with his estate. We were told that his funeral and other costs were being picked up by the government. What is it that we have to do?"

"Legal issues? Not sure…unless it's the deed. But that's been taken care of. The son, a Mr…let me see, Sawyer, William Sawyer, signed the last of those and sent them back yesterday. It's all taken care of." Mr. Cass smiled at them both. "You want me to read you the will?"

Payton put his hand on Sydney's arm when he could feel her anger boiling over. He didn't understand either why they were here, but neither of them had gotten a lot of sleep over the past few days and this guy was being dense.

"Maybe you could tell us why we're here. We have some things that require our attention elsewhere and we need to get going."

Payton and Sydney were meeting with Devin Grant to sign the papers on the pre-adoption of baby Cooperider. Devin told them last night that they would need a name by then. The birth certificate they had been give just said Baby Girl 1245. The number after her name signified how many nameless babies they had at this time.

"Sure, I understand. Gotta take care of the little one. Let's see. Okay. Well, basically, he left everything to you, Miss Waite. There was the house in Louisiana that he sold recently and that has been amended. Then there was the one he purchased recently, plus the estate of his—"

"Wait. I don't understand. He left me…What are you saying? I'm his heir? That can't be right. I know he had an ex-wife and I think a son. They…I don't understand." Sydney looked over at him and he reached for her hand. The baby started fussing and Payton put the pacifier in her mouth. It wouldn't quiet her for long, she hated the thing, but it would keep her quiet for a bit longer.

"Yes, his son William Sawyer has signed his portion over to you as well. He didn't know his biological father and wanted nothing to do with him or his estate. Mr. Shipley's mother passed on about ten years ago and his father was never in the picture either." Mr. Cass handed Sydney a file. "It's all in there. The deed to the houses, the money in the accounts. He had some investments that I've changed over to your name. His estate will pay for my fees. Mr. Shipley was a very savvy business man. He did know his way around a legal document. Like I said, he had everything laid out for you. I believe there's a letter in there as well."

Sydney stood up and began pacing. Payton didn't know why, but that made him nervous. She was flipping through the file and muttering under her breath. He heard the words "jackass" and "cocksucker" a few times then he heard her say "mother fuck" before she sat down and addressed the lawyer.

"It says here that he was worth over eight million dollars. That can't be. He was always broke. Hell, he owed me thirty bucks when I got shot. How can he be worth that much?"

Mr. Cass laughed slightly. "I assure you, he was. And that's just the properties and monies he had. There are several investments that he also had. Again, all those are now in your name. I would estimate his net worth to be right around fifteen million, give or take on the market."

"Shit," Payton said softly. "Fifteen mill and the kid of his just turned it over to Sydney? Why?"

"That's what I asked him. He said that he'd made it this far without anything from him and it would be very hypocritical of him to take anything from him now." The lawyer looked down at a file on his desk. "The boy was adopted not long after the divorce. Could be this other man raised him to be a good kid."

Sydney went to the car seat and pulled out the baby. She held her tight and looked at him. She had the most beautiful smile, Payton thought.

"Tell me Mr. Cass, do you happen to know Shipley's mother's name?"

"Yes, I do. Let me look here…"

About the Author

Hello! My name is Kathi Barton and I'm an author. I have been married to my very best friend Sonny for at times seems several lifetimes – in a good way, honey. And together we have three wonderful children and then the ones we brought into the world - Paul and Dale Barton, Jason and Wendy Barton and Danielle and Ben Conklin. They have given us seven of the greatest treasures on Earth. They don't live at home seven days a week! No, seriously, seven grandchildren – Gavin, Spring, Ben, Trinity, Sarah, Kelly and Kian.

www.ingramcontent.com/pod-product-compliance
Lightning Source LLC
Chambersburg PA
CBHW020600180626
46810CB00007B/2581